CONQUERING WHITNEY

A Mountain of Misadventure

BY BLAINE LANGBERG

Critical Eye Publishing
Farmington, Minnesota

Edited by D.J. Schuette
www.criticaleyeediting.com

Critical Eye Publishing
Farmington, MN 55024

CRITICAL EYE

Visit the author at www.blainelangberg.com.

For Ariel, Juliette, and Shira

PREFACE

Dear Reader,

While some of you may know me as the author of *Journey of a JuBu: How a Neurotic Jew Found His Inner Bu,* I'm also an orthodontist and comedian. I want to explain how this dichotomy works in my life. I find pleasure in both the scientific part of my brain *and* the part that is creative and determined to captivate and engage my audience—even (and maybe especially) when my writing distorts my adventures into a new imagined realm. While the scientist/doctor part of me is drawn to concrete truths as they relate to time and place—like the California sunlight paving my way up a steep climb or the precise elevation of a given mountain as I explore its reaches—the storyteller in me searches for humor. I look for it within everyday anecdotes from my past as a nerdy Jewish kid growing up in Westchester County, New York, and in my life experiences as a father, husband, and orthodontist.

The idea for this memoir originated after I began reading my journals from prior travels and thought they were an entertaining story. I then had an epiphany—I would write an autofiction travel narrative through the eyes of Jacob Silverstein, the primary character of my first book, *Journey of a JuBu*. I was suddenly excited for the challenge of writing an engaging, funny, and meaningful book without Jacob's comical and sometimes exasperating alter-ego, Adam Freeman!

Although I've been writing about Adam since 2008, his neurotic personality and petty antics became harder and more challenging for me to bottle up in novel form. Writing out snippets of Adam-esque stories and sharing them with audiences became more fun, thus launching my comedy career in 2017. Comedy allows me to laugh at myself and find the humor in life. Late nights connecting with diverse audiences in suburban playhouses in Connecticut, New York City comedy clubs, or bars in Maine adds another important layer to my writing. When writing this novella based on my journal entries, I imagined doing a Moth show, my audience in a dark room, eating appetizers and sipping cocktails while they listen to stories from my life that I hope feel as particular and human as they do epic and universal.

While it may seem like some of my characters have regressed at points during my writing journeys, this trip up Mt. Whitney came before I learned about the mind-body connection and meditation. The chapters that follow are from past travels when I was more a neurotic Jewish person than a mindful Buddhist. I consider this my prequel—my "pre-Bu" phase of life.

May you, my Readers, be healthy, happy, and peaceful.

Your JuBu friend,
Blaine Langberg

Chapter 1 – Headlamps

Darkness engulfs me. The trail is indistinguishable in the night. Glancing at my cell phone, I see it's 3:00 a.m.; sunrise is still four hours away. My heart pounds—adrenaline courses through my body. I've never done anything like this before in my life.

I turn on my headlamp (which my wife's family unflatteringly calls a "dork light") to illuminate the way. The rocky Californian terrain is very different from the more familiar dirt paths I hike on my home turf in Connecticut.

Mark, our guide, cinches my backpack tighter around my waist. Barlow, one of my oldest buddies from dental school, takes a swig of water from his Camelback. Being with these bros makes me feel like an honorary member of 5:30 Nation, their self-proclaimed early-morning workout club. For most of my life, I've felt like an outsider, never belonging to any one tribe (unless you count being Jewish), but this new sense of camaraderie forces a deep breath through my nose, the air expanding my lungs and dissipating some of the jangling in my nerves.

While hiking local trails has always been a cathartic experience for me, never in my wildest dreams did I imagine I'd find myself standing at the base of Mt. Whitney in the early hours of a chilly, late-October morning, about to hike 21.5 miles in a single day. I turn to Barlow to see if his eyes reflect the same fear of hiking up 14,500 feet as I'm sure mine do, but he quickly puts his hands up, shielding his eyes from my blinding headlight, then turns his head away.

Mark breaks the deafening silence. "You fellas ready?"

I glance at my cell phone one last time before we begin. No bars.

"We don't get cell phone reception here?" I ask.

Mark laughs. "What did you think, Jacob? We're on a mountain in Lone Pine, California, in the middle of nowhere."

Despite the cold, I feel sweat gathering under the bill of my New York Yankees cap. "What if my wife needs to get in touch with me? Or an emergency happens at my office?"

Mark looks at me, head cocked at an angle, the light from his headlamp shining on my green Patagonia jacket. "Even if you *had* service, do you really think you could help someone from here?"

I start to reply, but he cuts me off: "That was obviously a rhetorical question."

Mark certainly doesn't mince words. I appreciate him giving it to me straight, but the anxiety is still there. "What if someone gets into an accident while we're hiking? Remember *Into Thin Air*? A guy broke his leg climbing Mt. Everest. Or what about Reese Witherspoon when she gets hurt on her hike along the Pacific Coast Trail in *Wild*."

"You're nuts, Silverstein!" Barlow chimes in. We have the habit of addressing each other by our last names. "We're not climbing Everest, and Witherspoon's character hiked by herself. Plus, those are movies."

"Yeah, but they're based on true stories!" I snap back. "And they were both books first."

Clearly, 5:30 Nation isn't the most well-read bunch, but before I say anything else, Mark pats his backpack. "Either way," he says, "We're cool. The sat phone is in here if we need help. Besides, it'll be good to disconnect for a day."

"Right," Barlow says and takes another sip of water from his Camelback.

They have a point. No electronics to preoccupy my brain as we climb the mountain. Only the trail, my supplies, and

Mother Nature (along with Barlow and Mark, of course) will accompany me on this trip. No outside noise. No distractions.

I'm used to fifteen texts before breakfast, checking twenty unread emails at lunch, and getting worked up over an alert that my fantasy football team lost before dinner. Not being held hostage to constant notifications should have felt like heaven, but where would my brain go when my lungs burned and my legs ached?

"Let's go!" Mark motions us forward. His signal saves me from more incessant worry.

We are off!

Little rocks crunch beneath my hiking boots as we begin our ascent. I fumble with the new hiking poles Mark lent me before we began. "You'll thank me later," he'd said. "The poles will take pressure off your knees and help you balance." Now, with minimum visibility, his words ring prophetic—the poles keep me from toppling over, and thank God my trusty dork light illuminates where it's safe to step as I concentrate on NOT rolling my ankle on a loose rock. No time to check out the scenery—if I can even call it that in the mottled dark. No time to communicate as we move along the ridged path. Each of us are entrenched in our own version of the moment, of breathing and keeping our balance on this "extreme hike," when, just six months ago, I didn't even know what an extreme hike was.

Over the next twelve hours, every part of my body would come to comprehend what "extreme hike" meant. I would soon be scrambling over rocks and testing my limits physically and mentally as I struggled with my relationship to my inner child. In the hours that followed, each segment offered a new battle of will, sending me deeper into my past to make sense of the present.

Chapter 2 – The Emperor

The seed for Mt. Whitney was first planted by Barlow—*Andy Barlow*—whom I'd admired since we met as residents at Harvard. Barlow, three years older than me, was tall, dark, handsome, and a super charismatic dude. He always lit up a room with his contagious energy, and he was one of those people who did everything in half the time everyone else did. Although dental school was stressful (at the age of twenty-six I started using Just for Men to hide my premature gray hair), nothing phased Barlow. He not only graduated from dental school at the top of his class, but more impressively, he did so with a full head of glistening brown hair.

Once, at lunch, he blurted out that he had been an emperor in a past life. After I got done laughing, I asked him what the hell he was talking about.

"My wife dragged me to see her psychic last week. She said I should be careful not to abuse my power in this life like I did when I was an emperor in Egypt."

I laughed again. "You believe that?"

"Sure, why not?" he said, struggling to keep a straight face. "Isn't it obvious I was an emperor in another life? I mean look at my skill set: president of my class in dental school; speaker at my upcoming orthodontic graduation; admissions officer for incoming residents…."

At that time, I was in the process of applying to an orthodontic residency at Harvard, so I didn't argue with him; as the admission's officer, he was my ticket to learning how to straighten teeth.

Nearly two decades later, it was still a funny image: Barlow ruling a kingdom in his previous life, like Khaleesi in *Game of Thrones*, his charisma drawing countless followers into this Empire of Bros. Now, here I was, suddenly among the adoring masses after Barlow had invited me to join his epic 5:30 Nation—a group of super-buff dudes who met at 5:30 every morning to train on Newport Beach while reinventing CrossFit in the process. His boys were avid runners, cyclists, and swimmers—triathletes challenging themselves with intense workout sessions. According to Barlow, their most recent bonding experience entailed a rim-to-rim run of the Grand Canyon, and now, as an encore, they planned to conquer Mt. Whitney, the highest mountain in the contiguous forty-eight states.

"Most people camp out overnight before they summit," Barlow said, "but we're doing an *extreme* hike—climbing to the top and down in a day."

I pictured him and his buddies as a clan of broad-chested, strong-shouldered dudes giving bro-hugs and high fives after their workouts. Members of 5:30 Nation, with rippling back muscles and tennis ball-shaped calves, would march up Mt. Whitney single-file like they were on a special-ops mission. It didn't take long for me to realize that, unlike Barlow's bros, who drank scotch on the rocks, drove fast cars, and frequented cigar bars where they made billion-dollar venture capital deals to fund start-up companies, I was just a scrawny Jewish guy from Connecticut who preferred drinking orange soda and binging on Doritos while watching *The Big Bang Theory* over extreme exercise any day.

At first, I couldn't fathom accompanying them. In my mind's eye, I imagined 5:30 Nation gallivanting leagues ahead of me up the mountain, long before I'd finished tightening my hiking boots. And yet, another part of me was deeply curious about what it would mean to join their tribe, even if it (or I) was short-lived. When Barlow first told me over the phone how "totally stoked" he was to hike Mt. Whitney, I felt a pang of longing, awakening my wounded inner child. The picked-on kid—chosen last in every elementary school kickball game—felt like I could never handle such a hike. But adult me was determined to counter this doubting voice, because I know confronting discomfort lays at the heart of growth.

Barlow explained that none of the other 5:30 guys had ever climbed Whitney before, taming my anxiety. They were bringing in a new member to lead the expedition—Mark— who'd already summited Mt. Whitney three times! Barlow also said there was no "technical" climbing, which meant we wouldn't need ropes and harnesses to scale the mountain, and that we would follow a clearly marked trail. Music to my ears, and I told my inner child so: "See, everyone's on a level playing field. We can hang with the cool kids for once."

But my inner child still scoffed: *Those tanned alpha males are the polar opposite of you!*

"Stop being so snarky," I told him.

I mean, honestly, look in the mirror. You're a pasty-white, self-proclaimed nerd!

My inner child wasn't wrong, but I was getting pretty tired of listening to the self-loathing masochist whose only goal was to tear me down quicker than I could take a full breath. The wisest part of me knew it was time to put the subconscious, self-sabotaging voice to the test and prove it wrong. Without another thought, I texted Barlow, telling him I'd join their ranks.

He sent me a thumbs-up followed by: *details to follow.*

And just like that, over the lighthearted premise of a text message chain, I committed myself to a life-altering journey. I still wonder what the hell I was thinking. What was I trying to prove? And yet, as much as every part of me wanted to back out (it wasn't too late to say I'd forgotten a family trip or an orthodontic conference), the better part knew that if I didn't try to *keep up*, it would haunt me.

Forever.

Chapter 3 – Convincing Schmoopy

After I took the leap and agreed to join 5:30 Nation's extreme hike up Mt. Whitney, a smile the length of the Grand Canyon stretched over my face. I scampered into the kitchen, where my wife was on her cell phone doing the *New York Times* crossword puzzle.

She looked up. "Look at you, beaming. Did the Yankees win the Super Bowl or something?"

Leah has a lot of interests, but sports aren't among them. "The Yankees are baseball, and they would play in the World Series. The Giants are my football team, and the Super Bowl isn't until the beginning of February, Schmoopy," I say, using the endearing, Seinfeldian pet name for my wife to soften her up.

Leah suspected something immediately, "Okay, so what's with the shit-eating grin?" I looked around to make sure the kids weren't in earshot. Leah knew what I was thinking. "They're playing downstairs. Don't worry, they didn't hear me swear."

"If they did, you owe them another five bucks each," I told her playfully. "Do you kiss your parents with those filthy lips?"

She put down her phone, got up, and walked over to me. "No, but I do kiss *you* with these dirty lips. You've never seemed to mind." As if to prove it, she leaned in and planted one on me.

"True!" I said after we finally separated. "I just spoke with Barlow and—"

"How's The Emperor doing?" she asked.

"He's good. I just agreed to go on a hike with him and his buddies in October."

Leah backed away in surprise. "Seriously?"

Reality hit just about as hard as Leah's reaction. I was not in my twenties anymore, free to plot my life according to the whims of my ego. I mean, I had responsibilities—a family to support and an orthodontic practice to run. But Leah and I were also not attached at the hip, and we did things apart on occasion. My wife's not the controlling type, but I realized I probably should have asked her to sign off on the trip before committing. There was no denying that my wife's approval was *logistically* way more important than Barlow's. It appeared it was going to take more effort than expected to get my overworked and under-supported wife on board.

"I'm sorry. It was a weird conversation and I…um, kind of committed to hiking up Mt. Whitney with Barlow and his friends. That's okay, right?"

Leah sat back down, picked up her phone, and continued her crossword. "Is it a big hike?"

"Whitney's in California, the tallest mountain in the contiguous forty-eight states. Are you okay with it?"

Leah looked up from her phone. Based on the look on her face, it was *not* okay.

I dove deeper. "What's wrong?"

"Do you really think you can handle a climb like that? It sounds dangerous."

"I hike."

She giggled. "Yeah, once a month, on a little local trail in Matingly, Connecticut! What you're talking about is a different animal. For real hikers."

"What? I'm a real hiker!" I responded defensively with my arms flailing around.

Leah bent her head down, trying to hide her smirk. My sarcastic wife strikes again. "I'm teasing. Sure, you love to hike, but this sounds intense. My friend's cousin hiked Mt.

Kilimanjaro, and he trained for *six months*. What will *you* do?"

"Well, this isn't Kilimanjaro, but point taken. I should step up my training. Things are crazy between work and home, but I can manage."

Leah got back up and crossed the room, grabbed a box of pasta from the pantry, and filled a pot with water. "How long would you be gone?"

"Maybe three or four days." Then I saw it—the hurt in her eyes that Dr. Tina, our couple's therapist, was teaching me to look for.

"You're upset I didn't check with you before agreeing to go, aren't you?"

"No.... Yeah. You know it's important to me that you think about *us* before thinking about yourself. I feel hurt."

How would Dr. Tina advise me to handle this situation? I walked over to her, placed the pot on a stove burner, and turned it on. "I apologize, Leah. I wanted to do something healthy and positive for myself."

"For yourself? Like going to concerts and sporting events and taking writing courses? And now you're going to train for a guys' trip up a very tall mountain? You get plenty of time to yourself, especially while I'm running this house!" Leah picked at her right index finger. After a quiet second, she mumbled a curse, grabbed a tissue, and dabbed her cuticle to staunch a welling drop of blood.

She was right, as always, and this was not our first rodeo. This discussion had played on repeat throughout the years, but now I am trying to be more attuned to Leah and our girls.

I walked into this conversation thinking I could express my point of view in a sincere and genuine way, and I inevitably wound up feeling selfish and narrow-minded. While I am generous with my time with patients and staff at work, I still try to save energy for home—I want to be the best husband and father I can be. But a lot of days, my battery is dead by the time I walk in the door. Maybe the hike was less about wanting time away with the guys to bro out and more about giving myself some true alone time to reflect, reenergize, and recharge in nature. Maybe it was hard for Leah to understand that when she felt like *she* never got time to reflect, re-energize, and recharge.

It didn't matter, though. Leah insisted on getting to the heart of the matter. "I feel like this is the Turkey Trot all over again. Two months of intense training…all the family time you sacrificed…just for a 5k. Dinners missed, early morning workouts…. You were so tired from running in the morning that you fell asleep at Rina's violin concert. It was embarrassing."

"I hear what you're saying."

"I'm frustrated and worried I'll be a single mom again while you're off at the gym. I want you here for meals. Studies have shown that families who eat together are less likely to have children who become drug addicts later."

I winced, not seeing how my Mt. Whitney hike would lead to a heroine crisis for our kids, but my wife could dart down random rabbit holes faster than anyone I knew. What I thought was an easy request had flown off the rails. I tried to focus the "discussion" back on the actual hike. "Honey, I spend all day taking care of my patients. Mt. Whitney's a way for me to rest and challenge myself."

She looked into my eyes, "Sounds like you've already made up your mind. You really want to do this, don't you?"

"Yes." I paused a beat. "I'm sorry I didn't check with you first—I was desperate to join the trip…but you're right, I put myself ahead of the family. I like Barlow, and I like the whole idea of this journey. I thought I could be one of the cool kids for once in my life."

In the silence that followed, a vague memory from kindergarten flashed through my mind—I wanted to play Hungry Hungry Hippos with the other kids, but they ignored me. Out of spite, I swallowed a marble from their game, but then a classmate told our teacher, who rushed me to the school nurse. I was sent home, and my parents were instructed to sift through my poop for the marble. My parents were livid ("How could you be so selfish, Jacob!"), and something about that word, "selfish," stayed with me, haunting me evermore.

I stared into my wife's eyes, into the silence she refused to break. Until she did.

"If it means that much to you...."

I leaned closer to her as I anxiously waited for her answer.

"Okay."

I gave her a big kiss on the lips. She blushed. "Thanks, Leah."

A wave of relief washed over me, and I promised myself I'd let go of little Jacob and the poop marble forever. Maybe I'd been chasing an unselfish, sacrificial life (living for my wife, work, and family commitments), but I needed this for me. Maybe being selfish once in a while was okay at this point in my life. But, out of respect for Leah and the kids, I still needed to find a way to honor my family commitments.

"You'll see," I told her. "I won't go overboard with the training this time. You can even sign off on my schedule, Schmoopy!"

Leah grabbed the salad bowl and veggies from the fridge. As she cut the vegetables, I stood behind her, braiding her straight, bleach-blonde hair. She loves when I do that. But her rigid body told me she was still skeptical. I wrapped my arms around her, and after a minute, I felt her body relax into me.

"Okay," she said again. "But remember, family time comes first. The kids love our Soup Sundays and Taco Tuesdays together." She turned to face me, then her eyes narrowed, and her mouth stretched into a playful grin. "Oh yeah! While this little talk is fresh in your mind…. I forgot to tell you that I booked a cruise with my girlfriends in July, HunBuns," she said, turning my own strategy against me. "You're good with that, right?"

There it is, I thought. I had played right into her trap, but it still felt good to know we were both taking time for ourselves…even though I hardly knew what was in store for me three months later. While Leah swept the cut vegetables into the salad bowl, I pictured myself standing at the base of Mt. Whitney like that small boy pleading to play Hungry Hungry Hippos.

Chapter 4 – Hans and Franz

Two hours in, and somehow, miraculously, I'm still holding my own. Mark is at my twelve o'clock, leading the way, and Barlow is at my six. Their close proximity keeps my fearful inner voice quiet as our boots crunch steadily over twigs and stones.

Sunlight streams through the trees, sharp shadows slipping between root and brush. We're approaching the majestic Lone Pine Lake, glassy water pricked with orange and golden light I've only ever seen in my guidebooks. A half hour ago, we were walking along an elevated string of logs bridged above a creek. Although the trail leveled out, the ground is rocky and rigid. Lone Pine Lake's beauty distracts from the challenge of traversing this new terrain.

The sun beats harder, and Mark turns around, halting our hike in front of the lake. He strips off a layer, and a muffled, "It's getting hot!" escapes his mouth.

"I'm sweating my balls off!" Barlow retorts, cupping his crotch.

I wouldn't have put it quite as eloquently, but then again, I don't have his flare for drama. We all cut a quick layer without wasting any time.

In one graceful motion, Mark swings his backpack around and snags an energy bar. Barlow's eating his trail mix as Mark assures us we are making good progress. He glances at his Garmin. "The other group started already, so we've got to keep moving."

Mark insisted on climbing in two groups to create a check-and-balance system. Our triad of slower hikers (thanks to me and Barlow) were given a head start. The other five faster hikers would eventually catch up with us so we could summit together as a team.

"There's a lot more mountain ahead, boys," Mark says, cheering us on. "Let's go!"

I take a moment to imprint the image of the pristine Lone Pine Lake in my mind. The pictures online don't do the lake justice. I soak in the reflection of the mountains in the crystal-clear water. I'm mesmerized by what should surely be a professional photograph: the mountains framed by the sky above and the lake below with the golden sunrise highlighting the still water. I haven't felt this much joy since my youngest daughter, Autumn, was born. Thinking of her makes me wish my family could experience the peace and harmony I feel. Words can't articulate this life-portrait of Mother Nature. I grab my phone and snap a picture to at least capture the moment for my family.

I plop down on top of a large, flat rock and take a deep breath that cleanses my soul. I release an audible "haaaaa," letting go of so much more than just excess air.

"Silverstein! Time to move along," Barlow hollers as he and Mark peel out onto the trail.

I fumble to put my phone away and rush to fall in line behind Mark. He's built like a damn tank and has the confidence of the British adventurist Bear Grylls. I watch as he takes a swig from his Nalgene water bottle without missing a beat or spilling a drop. He's a bulldog full of patience and calm—the perfect guide so far. I feel completely at ease as we inch closer to the top with each step. Is it possible that all will continue as peaceful, patient, and calm as it's been thus far?

Another hour passes, and my breathing is heavier and my steps slower as we make our way from Lone Pine Lake to Mirror Lake. I planned to tune out conversation with music, but social graces have kept me chatting with Mark and Barlow throughout the trek. Thankfully, they're now twenty feet ahead, embroiled in a Pearl Jam-versus-Nirvana debate, giving me the perfect moment to plug in. Headphones on, check. Music playing, check. Engaged in my blissful alternative-rock hiking mix, check.

"On your left," I hear someone with a heavy German accent yell. I turn my head and see two twenty-something, muscle-bound bodybuilders approach, both with short black hair. In nylon shorts, T-shirts, and with Poland Spring water bottles in their hands, they appear to be underdressed and ill-prepared. They aren't even lugging backpacks!

I put my headphones back in my pocket. The mountain air inspires me to engage them in conversation. "Good morning," I blurt.

"Morning," they reply in unison, passing me.

The silence on the mountain is deafening. I walk quicker and catch up to chat with these strangers. When I ask the German versions of Hans and Franz from *Saturday Night Live* what brought them here, the Franz doppelganger says, "We travel across California. We thought cool to hike."

"Wow, so you're doing the extreme hike?"

He looks confused. "Extreme hike? No understand. We...how you say...discovered Whitney. Decided climbing would be fun."

I'm impressed with his English and spirit of adventure, but I can't get over their light hiking attire and lack of gear. Even outfitted with all my Patagonia and North Face clothes, am I an imposter? These dudes seem like they're out for a leisurely morning stroll along the Rhine River. Maybe the mountain isn't as tough to summit as I thought it would be. I feel myself spiraling, taking a 180-degree turn from the peaceful perch on the flat rock at Lone Pine Lake. I try to refocus.

"Are you guys concerned you'll have a hard time making it to the top?"

They both shrug. Franz, obviously the spokesman of the two, says, "We research…is okay." I lengthen my strides to keep up with their pace. They start to push ahead of me, and I can barely hear him. He turns back, and I catch "…we're in good shape. Should not be problem."

In his own strong German accent, the short one, Hans, wisely (or smart-assily) adds, "You enjoy journey. Bye-bye."

As the Germans fade from my view, I'm left alone to think. My legs and thoughts are heavy as I trudge up the rocky trail.

Did I overprepare for this trip? Is it just my nature to spin, spiral, and go non-stop? Was my effort even worth it? My headphones stay in my pocket as I continue to ponder, wonder, regret, and chatter for the next mile or so, unable to keep a quiet mind and enjoy the present.

Chapter 5 – Gym Rat

The Germans, about forty feet ahead of me now, move past Barlow and Mark. I increase my pace like a toddler trying to keep step with their parents, and I flash back to my prep for this adventure.

I started my training like a soldier preparing for battle. I didn't want to be the runt of the litter, a singled-out burden left in the dust. I was in good shape when I enlisted with the 5:30 Nation, running a couple miles a few times a week to stay fit and sane. Being serious about the summit, though, meant I had to dust off my treadmill and lean into cardio like my wife leans into new episodes of *The Real Housewives of Beverly Hills.*

With a cock of the head and a hint of a smirk tugging at her lips, Leah said, "You must really be serious about this," when I passed her in the kitchen with a red rag and an old bottle of Endust spray.

"What do you mean?" I asked.

"In twelve years of marriage, I've never seen you clean *anything*. You should train to climb Mt. Everest next year too. At least the house will be immaculate."

The next step was adding a gym membership into our monthly budget. At first, Leah was reluctant about me joining the Town Rec Center, insisting that the initiation fee combined with the membership seemed overboard, but I showed her my OCD-organized, weight-training Whitney prep binder to secure her blessing. Maybe she saw my desperate, childlike need to make this happen and put my wounded inner child to bed for good. I don't know if she was excited for me or pitied me, but either way she co-signed the gym plan with me.

I started logging reps in my binder, every bit as meticulous as when Leah tracked our firstborn's bowel movements. Most of the time, I felt like the buff teenagers in the free-weight section were going to tell me I didn't belong there, but thankfully, I fit in as a new gym rat. I wasn't flexing my muscles in the mirror for Facebook-worthy selfies, but then again, these kids weren't tracking their reps in an old-school binder. After each rep, I slumped on the bench, bare-bones, no spotter, taking at least fifty pounds off the load these Terminator-style teens were lifting.

Taking all their weight off the barbell grew tiring, so it wasn't long before I found myself in the back of the gym hiding near the Nautilus machines and sixty-year-olds. The safety locks, adjustable knobs, and geriatric crowd provided comfort.

When I followed Grandpa Henry on the shoulder press and still had to lower the weight (in my defense, he'd been working out since his thirties), I almost gave up, but I would not be proven wrong after coming this far. I got through a full three sets of shoulder presses and kept coming back after that. Eventually, the old-timers accepted me as their new trainee, and my persistence even paid off with the cool college kids, who finally started making eye contact with me as they flexed in front of the mirror.

When I asked a twenty-year-old kid named Cole to spot me—and he did—my mission was accomplished. I'd earned some major gym cred just weeks away from my Mt. Whitney adventure. A few days before I left, Cole and his gym bros even asked for my Insta handle so they could follow me. After they explained what Insta was, and after I quickly created an account, they told me they wanted a pic of me at the summit. They would be following me on IG, after all. I was finally shedding my outsider inner child and embracing a sense of bravado I'd never known before.

My hiking poles help propel me along, but I'm losing ground on my new German hiking friends. They're now hundreds of feet ahead of Mark and Barlow, and I couldn't feel further away, like a fuzzy, distant memory. I feel like a tagalong kid. *The Emperor would rather have those Germans alongside him than me trailing behind like a puppy dog.* At this pathetic pace, I'll summit Mt Whitney alone, if at all. Gym rat training with Cole, Grandpa Henry and his geriatric crew, and my gym binder were all for nothing; I'm barely hanging on.

Then I remember the mantra I wrote inside my binder: *Be Prepared. Put in the work. It'll pay off!* I *am* prepared. I *did* the work. I *can do* this! With positivity pulsating through my body, I pull myself up by the bootstraps and remember I'm not taking selfies for anyone other than me (and maybe Cole and friends). Right now, this is my Mecca. I buckle up, lengthen my strides, and quicken my steps. Those German blokes have nothing on me. I, too, can be spontaneous and embrace the thrill of adventure. I, too, can summit this mountain. I let the spirit of Whitney fill my core. I imagine the expansive view and the freedom and power of it all at the top and quicken my pace again.

Even after a twenty-minute sprint, I can no longer see the Germans. I'd hoped to prove that I could hang with the frosty, accidental travelers, but they're long gone. They have left me in the dust. I'm obsessing over them, their stamina and strength, and my, well...*lack* of all those things when Barlow and Mark come back into view.

I take a deep breath of clean mountain air. Why am I comparing myself to other people again? I need to go at my own pace and follow my own path. All will be well if I concentrate on the moment at hand and release my fear of belonging. All will be well if I let go of my worry about summiting with the 5:30 Nation. Forget about the destination and enjoy the journey, Jacob Silverstein!

Chapter 6 – Under the Domes

Mark and Barlow wait for me as I scurry into Trail Camp, where yellow and blue dome tents pop like smiling emojis out of an otherwise barren, monochromatic wasteland. The dome-shaped tents feel like cheating at this point—for those who don't have it in them to hike the mountain in a day and decide, instead, to spend the night. It's quiet, peaceful, as campers rest and refuel inside their bubbles. As I forge toward them, I notice the brown dirt path has turned a rockier gray, and the soaring green trees at the base of the trail feel like a distant memory as I scramble over bonsai-looking shrubs and knee-high succulents that thrive in this climate.

I come to a halt in front of my 5:30 Nation brethren. They each give me a fist bump while I quickly take out my water bottle to quench my thirst. Mark breaks the silence.

"Here we are fellas," he says. "Six miles in the books! We're more than halfway there. He looks up and points to the mountainside in front of us. "Check it out!"

"The ninety-seven switchbacks! Just a few more miles to Trail Crest," Barlow says, stating the obvious. I wonder if he's speaking to me, the novice, in particular. Regardless, he's clearly pumped about ascending the final 2500 feet to the summit.

"I read about that," I say curtly, wiping the sweat off my upper lip before anyone can sense my nerves over the words "ninety-seven switchbacks."

"It's legendary." Barlow punches me on the arm. "I'm stoked! The real ascent's about to start, bro!"

My mind flips through images of the infamous switchbacks I saw on YouTube as prep for the hike—the ever-increasing steepness, the dizzying zig-zags.... I almost feel nauseous. Though all the online guides claim that the switchbacks are a friend—a way to counterbalance the vertical ascent by snaking around it—I am not a snake, and the thought of constantly switching directions for the next two-plus miles sounds like an upside-down rollercoaster for my nervous system. And I'm feeling weaker rather than stronger (and definitely less confident) the higher we get.

Out of the corner of my eye, I see a bearded man step out of his yellow tent. I stand straighter and watch him sleepily put on his hiking boots. I've been up since the crack of dawn, climbing for six hours, and he's rubbing the tired out of his eyes. I pull my lats tighter, holding firm, as the yellow tent ruffles again and out comes a portly man holding the hand of a dark-haired, creamy-skinned child who looks a little younger than my seven-year-old daughter, Rina. The man releases his son's hand, bends down next to the fire, and stirs a steaming black pot of something that flashes past my periphery as Barlow points to them and says, "Look at that family. Reminds me of the time we camped out at Yosemite."

I'm surprised by the pang of regret lifting from my ribs, but I refuse to acknowledge it out loud and get defensive instead. "The only way I can get my girls to spend time with me in nature is by forcing them to go on a hike for Father's Day."

"My kids love hiking with me," Barlow counters. *Of course they do.* "We did the mountains outside of LA each weekend to help me prep for this trek."

It's a jab in the gut; Barlow lives the reality I can only dream of in my own life. While I get shamed for missing basketball games, school plays, and family dinners, Barlow has a whole clan supporting him. Everything always comes up roses for Barlow—*The Emperor*—who really *is* charmed. But I'm not bitter about it or anything!

We walk past camp, and I fixate on the dad and son high-fiving, then breaking down the yellow tent together. A team. It would be so cool to experience that with my own family. I shake my head to rid it of the thought and look at my feet, reminding myself that only the present matters. Faulkner retorts that what's past is never past—it's haunted—and then my literary reverie is interrupted by Mark shouting, "Time to hit it!"

My feet won't move.

"You okay, Jacob? You're looking a little pale." Mark is close enough to reach for my shoulder. I am stunned silent, dizzy, as I look up at the imposing path.

"Um, it's really high up there," I blurt.

"No shit, Sherlock. We're climbing a mountain," Barlow plays.

"I'm serious. I can't go up there! That drop-off is too steep."

Mark looks at me like I just told him I hate puppies, a perplexed wrinkle spreading across his brow. "Excuse me?"

Barlow steps in. "He's just fucking with us." I pause and catch Barlow's subtle head nod in my direction. "Aren't you, Silverstein?"

"He looks spooked," Mark says and tries to hand me a snack, but I shake him off. "You sure? You'll need energy for the switchbacks. We've got to keep pushing."

Barlow faces me with worry. "Silverstein, what's really going on? You look like you're going to lose your breakfast. Are you alright?"

"No...." I trail off to some unknown corner of my mind and feel myself falling backwards. I say a quick prayer to my Jewish God that I don't faint and smash my head on a jagged rock.

Chapter 7 – Snoopy and the Infinite Sky

I don't black out, but a wave of terror seizes my body. I stand paralyzed beneath the edge of the cliff wrapping around the mountain. Barlow stares at me, but I look away.

"Hey, Silverstein, you good?"

My brain knows we need to move, but my feet are still frozen in place. I can't give my companion an explanation; my throat's as dry as the Sahara Desert. I shake my head.

Barlow wraps his right arm over my shoulder and gently nudges me forward with his left. "Let's go, Silverstein."

I'm a living statue.

"Come on, man. You heard Mark. We need to get going." Barlow pushes me to move along. "You're like in a trance. Snap out of it!"

I whip around, put my hands on Barlow's chest, and shove him violently. "Lay off me!"

Barlow stumbles backwards and glares at me in shock. "Dude, what the fuck?" He regains his composure and holds his hands up, signifying that he comes in peace. "What's gotten into you?"

I ignore the stares from the Trail Campers. "Don't tell me to snap out of it!"

"Silverstein, you need to put your big-boy pants on and man up."

"Screw you, Barlow."

To defuse the rising tension, Mark steps to my side and gently puts his hand on my back, giving me a paternal pat. His touch calms me.

"Barlow, you go on ahead," Mark says. "We'll catch up."

"Okay." Barlow peers into my eyes, and I look away again. As if detecting my pain, he says, "Don't worry, you got this. Later, bro." Barlow attacks the trail with long strides and begins his ascent up the switchbacks.

Mark gives me his full attention. "What's really going on, Jacob?"

"He told me to '*Snap out of it.*' Fuck him."

His brow crinkles in confusion. "What?"

"That's *exactly* what my dad used to tell me when I would throw a tantrum as a kid."

"Oh," Mark responds. "I don't think Barlow meant anything by it, but I guess that hit a nerve, huh?"

I nod.

Mark continues with his hike-side, pop-psychological diagnosis. "Doesn't sound like your father was very nurturing. That must have been frustrating for you."

"Sure. I guess. I mean, he's a good guy. He was a great provider, but I couldn't stand it when he said that. It always made me feel like there was something wrong with me."

Mark sits down on a nearby boulder and motions for me to join him. "I get it. Dads can really do a number on you. Nothing was ever good enough for my dad. For me, it was my senior year at the football state championship game. I was the star running back." Mark thumps his chest. "I ran eighty yards on one play but was tackled one yard short of the endzone. I was gassed and asked coach for a breather. The QB scored the touchdown on that drive. I rushed for two hundred yards that game, but all my dad talked about on the ride home was how I should've been the one to score. He was an expert fault-finder. He told me that asking to be taken out of the game for that one play was a sign of weakness. Honestly, he ruined football for me. That's why I didn't play in college. I can barely watch the Rams without old wounds bubbling to the surface. Family fucks you up, am I right?"

I take a slow, deep breath, internalizing Mark's thoughts. "Yeah. Makes me wonder what kind of long-term damage I'm causing my own girls. I guess, like my dad, I'm *not* purposely trying to cause any, but it's unavoidable." I grab my stomach and Mark hands me an energy bar. I unwrap it, take a bite, and speak through a mouthful of chocolate and peanuts. "I bet my dad didn't even realize what he said bothered me."

"Tell me why that phrase triggers you."

I finish chewing and rehash the story to Mark. I consider leaning on brevity but lean into vulnerability instead:

I'm seven, perched on my mother's lap, sitting alongside my sister and dad on the beach chairs we brought from home—our tiny family compound carved out in the concrete jungle of New York City. We're patiently (and impatiently, in my case) waiting for the Thanksgiving Day Parade to start, which was on my parents' bucket list. The sun rises, bathing the cement and glass city in pink, orange, and gold. We're scrunched among the mass of people like sardines, and I squeeze my mom's hand a little tighter. Even on this frigid morning, my palms are sweaty.

Finally, after hours of waiting, a marching band makes their noisy, tooting approach, and the crowd rejoices, cheers, claps. This isn't so bad, *I think. Before I can release my vice-hold on my mom's hand, a hulking, white, floating object grabs my awed gaze.* "See that Snoopy balloon? Isn't it neat?" *Mom rubs my hand with affection.*

Snoopy stops in front of us. I know I'll remember this enormous balloon for the rest of my life. I feel small and overwhelmed at the sight of Snoopy against a skyscraper backdrop surrounded by an infinite blue sky. I feel dizzy. My mind wanders with strange thoughts: What would happen if the people holding the balloon's ropes let go? Where would Snoopy fly to? What if someone continued to hold the rope and was dragged along with Snoopy as he flew away? Was there an end to the vast sky somewhere? What is the meaning of this? Where do I fit in among the infinite space of it all? Do I even fit in?

"Damn dude, those are some deep thoughts for a seven-year-old," Mark interjects. I wonder if he'll check his watch, calculating how much longer I'll likely drone on with this story. But it feels important, and I'm grateful for Mark's openness, especially because I never expected this from him when we first met.

"Obviously, I'm interpreting this as an adult, but all I know is that I was scared to death they'd let Snoopy go, and he'd float off into space."

Mark laughs, and I look at him, stung. "Sorry," he says. "I just have this image of a little kid being terrorized by cute, adorable Snoopy. I look for the humor in things. It really helps to laugh at yourself."

I'm about to get defensive, but when I see the grin on Mark's face, I'm disarmed. "I guess you're right—it does seem funny now. But at the time I was petrified. I didn't know how to articulate my feelings, so I started bawling."

I finish the energy bar and wrap up the story. "My mom tried to calm me down, but I dug my head deep into her chest. She kept telling me I was safe, but I was crying hysterically, screaming for her to take me home. But, like a stuck truck in mud, we weren't going anywhere, smothered in the crowd as we were. When my mom didn't listen, I cried louder to get her attention. Finally, I leaned my head into her chest and bit her."

"You bit your mom's boob? Freud would have a field day with that!"

"Yeah, I did. She threw me into my dad's arms, furious. My dad had a short fuse and didn't tolerate crying. He yelled, 'Snap out of it before I really give you something to cry about!' I knew what that meant, so I stifled my sobs to avoid getting the wooden spoon when we got home. For the rest of the parade, I hung onto his neck with my eyes closed as Charlie Brown, Underdog, and the giant turkey sidled past."

Mark looks at me. "So, seeing the ninety-seven switchbacks must have given you the same feeling as watching those balloons at the Thanksgiving parade."

I turn away and wipe tears from my eyes.

"But you're not that kid anymore, Jacob." Mark stands up and motions for me to join him. "That kind of vastness makes us all feel small. And it's normal to have that sense of vertigo when you're looking straight up."

"I guess."

"Here's what you're going to do…." Mark pats my back again. "Don't look up, don't look down, or to the sides. Keep your eyes forward and put one foot in front of the other. Hell, you can even look at the rocks on the trail if you need to. C'mon, let's go summit this sucker."

I stand still. "I don't know, Mark."

"I know you're scared, but you've got this. You didn't come all this way to stop now."

Out of the corner of my eye, I notice the family's yellow tent is all packed up. The bearded dad snaps the folded tent to the top of his backpack and motions for his family to follow.

Dads and son waste no time falling in line; the boy slips in between his parents, and they start on the first switchback.

Mark nudges me forward. "You can do this! I'll stay behind you and get your back!"

I watch the boy as he turns the corner. If he can do it, I can too. I nod and move out in front of Mark.

I've finally managed to *snap out of it*. "Let's go!"

Chapter 8 – The Ninety-seven Switchbacks

Right foot, step; right arm, swing; hiking pole, spike in the ground. Left foot, step; left arm, swing; hiking pole, spike in the ground.

Step—swing—spike.

Step—swing—spike.

Step—swing—spike.

These three words become my mantra while ascending the switchbacks.

As I turn onto switchback twenty-four, Mark no longer has my back. I look up to find Barlow and Mark five switchbacks ahead of me. With each swerve in the trail, though it's getting harder and harder to catch my breath, I try not to think about anything except the next step. I congratulate myself for not having glanced at my watch, let alone my cell phone, for hours. (I realize there is no service, but old habits die hard!) Time stands still when faced with the perilous beauty of Mother Nature.

I'm taken out of my *Zen and the Art of Ascending Whitney* moment when I step next to a GoGurt squeeze pouch. Who would litter on this pristine mountain? I bend down to pick up the garbage.

"Damn, people are so disrespectful," I mutter under my breath, stuffing the trash in my backpack even as I risk falling further behind. Since I'm already paused, I grab my water bottle just long enough to notice the family who'd emerged from the yellow tent twenty-four switchbacks below—that *Modern Family* trio from the Trail Camp—in front of me, stopping for snacks.

I can't believe these guys. First, they cheat on the hike by camping overnight, and now they're littering, breaking the cardinal rule of campers: *Pack it in, pack it out—leave no trace that you were ever here.*

This family is driving me nuts. I stomp towards them, reaching for the empty GoGurt pouch in the pocket of my pack, about to give them a piece of my mind.

The bearded father sits on a boulder holding his hiking poles. The short and stout dad peels a banana for his son. I notice the kid putting a water bottle back in his blue JanSport backpack with the name "Casten" embroidered on the pouch in white lettering. Before I can look away, the boy makes eye contact with me. He waves and smiles, stopping me dead in my tracks.

My scowl morphs into a grin. "I like your backpack," I tell Casten as he approaches. "My youngest daughter has the exact same one, but hers is pink." I quickly put the litter away.

"My favorite color is blue."

"I see that!" I give him a high five. His dad comes over with the banana.

"Good afternoon," he says to me. "How's your hike going?"

When I look up, I can barely see Mark and Barlow, leagues ahead of me by now. I don't want to be rude and ignore him, but I also know I have to keep moving.

In the end, politeness wins. "It's all good," I say. "How's *your* trek going?"

"It's been slow," he says, "but fun. Right, Casten?" His son nods sheepishly.

Casten drops his banana on the dirt trail and starts bawling. The dad bends down and gives him a hug. "It's okay, bud." Casten continues to cry despite his father's soothing compassion. "It's okay, honey. Daddy has another one. Mike, we need another banana!"

"I'm on it, Ben!" Mike, Casten's bearded dad, swoops down from his perch on the rock, swiftly removing another banana from a Ziploc bag. He peels it and removes the stringy parts meticulously—like a surgeon—and hands it off to Casten. I smile after seeing how impressively this family handled their child's meltdown. There was no *snap-out-of-it* moment for Casten from his fathers. He might end up a well-adjusted adult.

My anger at them for littering is gone. My jealousy of their family hike while my kids are back in Connecticut watching TikTok videos evaporates. I admire Ben and Mike—not only are they taking their son on the journey of a lifetime but also, in the process, they're showing him compassion and instilling a spirit of adventure. This family is doing it the right way!

I bend down to address my new little friend on the mountain. "That banana looks tasty!" Casten gives me a smile. "I'm super impressed with your hiking skills, buddy! Keep going up this mountain!" He opens his arms up wide, and I bend down to give him a hug. We are all one now. I'm rooting for this family to summit the mountain. "Have a great journey, guys!"

"Thanks. You too!" Ben and Mike say in unison.

My hike up the switchbacks continues, and because of my inadvertent pit stop, Mark and Barlow are nowhere in sight. Before I know it, I'm at switchback fifty-six. I think I see Mark's red backpack, maybe twelve switchbacks above. It's hard to concentrate on anything else but walking, and I quickly get vertigo, so I put my head down to look at the ground.

I've been hiking for over an hour, and miraculously, I can't remember how I got here. All I know for certain is that at the first switchback, my breaths were steady. Inhales were slow and deep—four seconds in and eight seconds out. But now, I'm losing concentration on my breath, and my heart rate soars. My pace slows and my breathing quickens. I make a conscious effort to focus on each step, repeating my switchback mantra:

Step—swing—spike.

Step—swing—spike.

Step—swing—spike.

It helps. My thoughts become free of worry; there is only the doing, the pressing on.

I have fallen in line amongst a caravan of Boy Scouts on the trail. Although I'm surrounded by teenagers and their dads, it brings me a sense of calm knowing that we are all in this together. We share a common bond: being on this mountain, on this day, with the goal of conquering the ninety-seven switchbacks. We have formed our own human machine—like a train moving up a winding path. I am a cog in the wheel, keeping pace with the teenager ten feet in front of me and being a role model for the kid ten feet behind me.

I feel at peace with the mountain as I trek along the switchbacks. It's like I'm having an awakening—an epiphany—corny as it sounds, especially considering that I've never really been a religious person. On the trail, the usual anger and irritation I feel over small things, like my girls not bringing their dishes to the sink after eating, has been replaced by awe for the natural beauty of the mountain. The sun's rays penetrating my long-sleeve hiking shirt fill me with warmth, and the white clouds popping out like cotton balls from the horizon is like a big hug of joy from God or Mother Nature or whatever higher power is out there. The love coming from the Universe is more palpable with each step.

Thank goodness I have my personal space, because these religious thoughts make me literally laugh out loud. I might soon be mistaken for a crazy person or a delirious climber in need of help! Maybe I'm laughing because of the contrast I feel on the mountain relative to how I react any time my wife asks me to go with her to Friday night services at the temple. She knows the answer is going to be no, yet still she gets upset with me like the tune of a song she cannot change. While she finds endless community in synagogue—in socializing with strangers and meeting up with friends—the space fills me with a discomfort that makes me feel removed from myself.

It likely has something to do with my *bar mitzvah* when I was thirteen. To this day, I carry with me the crippling anxiety I felt when I had to chant unpunctuated, memorized Hebrew in a toneless voice before a crowd of family members and friends who were judging me. Contrary to expectation, I felt the farthest thing from "becoming a man" (what my rabbi wanted me to believe) as I stood before everyone in a custom navy-blue suit. I was so tall and narrow for my height, no suit off the shelf would fit me, and my mother wasn't going to have her child look "unkempt." Having all those eyes on me when my face was breaking out with acne felt more like a cruel joke passed down from Abraham, Isaac, and Jacob rather than following in their Jewish tradition. Worse, my voice was in the middle of shifting registers, cracking and screeching as I chanted my Torah portion. Along with my changing voice, I also couldn't control what was happening *down there*—and there is truly nothing worse than having an erection inside the thin pants of a suit before an entire congregation.

Yes, that was me, fulfilling Uncle Chuck's prophecy just before my reading: "You're going to do great, Jacob. Knock on wood!"

Somehow, I've made it to switchback ninety. *I know this.* I've been counting. Only seven to go! Maybe it's the endorphin high, but as tired and exhausted as my body should feel, it's instead totally rejuvenated. Although not super athletic by nature (I'm more fan than athlete), today I'm a kindred spirit with my favorite sport superstars. Like Derek Jeter, Eli Manning, and Jalen Brunson often do, I've saved my best performance for the big moment. Something beyond what I can articulate is keeping me going and helping me perform at a level beyond what I thought I was capable of. I feel like I'm disassociating and having an out-of-body experience. Another part of me—perhaps my psyche—is marching at my side and cheering me on, hyping me up to reach new heights, both literally and figuratively, as I keep plowing up the switchbacks.

I think I'm hallucinating when I see the German duo, Hans and Franz, from Lone Pine Lake approach. "Hey," I pant. "I remember you guys. What's going on?"

They stop in front of me, looking beyond exhausted, like MMA fighters in the third round, their breathing heavier than mine. "We go back," says Franz. "My friend bad. Mountain make him sick."

"You mean he has altitude sickness?" I ask.

"He feel horrible," he says, his breathing still ragged.

I click the front straps of my backpack, freeing my chest, and swing it off my back. "Here, take some of my trail mix and electrolytes," I say, reaching into my bag to hand them the supplies. As they gobble up the food, I can already see color returning to their faces.

"You are kind," says Franz. "Good luck with climb."

"Thanks. Safe travels with the rest of your journey." I sling my backpack over my shoulder and click the straps back together. Then I smile to myself, remembering the motto painted on the walls of the Rec Center gym where I painstakingly trained for this: *Proper preparation and planning prevents poor performance.*

When I turn around, I see the Germans descending the ninety-seven switchbacks. *Poor guys*, I think. As much as I admire their spontaneity, they simply didn't prepare, and now they're paying for it. Where they are weak, I feel stronger, eager to prove myself capable—not only for myself, 5:30 Nation, and my family, but now for Casten, his dads, *and* the Germans!

After the Germans have faded into the switchbacks, I realize this is the first time I've looked back to take in the view. I gaze over the ledge at the trail, faced with a straight vertical drop with no clear end in sight.

My glasses fog up with sweat from the heat of my own breath and brow. Suddenly, I can't stop thinking about how it would only take one tiny slip to fall instantly to my death. My stomach churns, and I want to vomit. Was this the sickness the Germans were talking about? Am I about to follow them involuntarily down the trail?

I hear Mark's voice echoing down from above. "Come on! You got this, Jacob!"

When I turn back to look up the mountain, I don't see the face that goes with the voice, but I keep squinting until I find two specks, Mark and Barlow, at the Trail Crest cheering me on.

"Let's go, Silverstein!" Barlow bellows.

The sound of the 5:30 Nation Boys is enough for me to forget my fear. I lengthen my strides for the final two switchbacks even as my breath won't settle. It feels like there's a hole in my lungs every time I breathe, no matter how deeply I try, no matter how desperate I am to catch and hold the air. Are my alveoli even working? Do holes beget holes, or is this what it's like to have COPD? This is the last thought

I have before I feel four arms wrap around me in a double-bro bear hug.

"Congratulations, brother! You did it! You conquered the ninety-seven switchbacks," Mark says. "Let's rest a minute before we hit the exposed bridge. It's a doozy!"

I pull away from the hug. "Wait. *What?*"

Chapter 9 – I Scream, You Scream…

I munch on my granola bar and stare at the brown Trail Crest sign next to me, then I take a moment to admire the view of the snaking switchbacks. And to think, I was at the bottom of that monstrosity only an hour ago. I sit like Rodin's The Thinker, alone with my thoughts, savoring the moment. The training and sacrifice I made to hike the mountain is paying off.

Two crows land a few feet in front of me, pecking on the crumbs of someone's old trail mix. Like New York City pigeons, they have no fear and approach me for food. I get up, moving slowly from sheer exhaustion, stretch my arms, and shoo them away. Surprisingly, I'm not sore. Maybe the adrenaline high is masking it. Or maybe it's the serenity of knowing the switchbacks are behind me instead of looming ahead. What a difference twenty-four hours makes. Cue my sigh of relief.

My thoughts roll back to yesterday. The 5:30 Nation three-car caravan traveled northeast five hours from Newport Beach to Lone Pine. U2 blared over the radio as we drove through rustic red rocks blazing in the sunny desert. When I stepped out of the car, my muscles were stiff and tired, my head spinning from anxiety. I was a wreck. Heavy eyelids fell on the whole crew. Upon checking into the hotel, I yearned for a few quiet minutes and maybe a quick nap, but our self-proclaimed hiking guide, Mark, wouldn't allow it. Like a pop quiz the teacher springs on the class before a weekend, Mark planned for us to go on a four-hour practice hike. We huddled around the parking lot as he announced, "It's essential for us to see the trail in daylight. We need to get acquainted with the mountain and the land and earn her respect before we trek." We understood his point (and his mantra was catchy!), but his idea was initially rebuked by a vocal minority.

Jack—Adonis, Iron Man triathlete, and wealthy-as-they-come investment banker—objected to the prep hike.

Thank you, God, Mother Nature, and Adonis Jack, I thought.

"Dude, forget about the hike now, let's go into the town of Lone Pine! We'll be on the mountain all day tomorrow. And I have a hankering for an ice cream sandwich that won't quit," he said.

Teddy, a dermatologist by day and comedian at night, smirked and chimed in, "I agree with Mark. We're all stiff and tired, Jack, but ice cream sandwiches aren't going to prepare us for Whitney like the practice hike!"

Our fearless leader declared, "Whatever we choose, it's done together."

When Jack announced that he would treat the group to ice cream sandwiches, there was no more debate about what we were doing first.

The group climbed into Jack's Ford F-150 to hunt for ice cream sandwiches. Mark, with Teddy as his concierge, lobbied for a post-snack practice hike, and everyone solemnly swore like boy scouts to an abbreviated, two-hour trek.

Our first stop in Lone Pine was at Scoop, There It Is, the local ice cream shop where there was not an ice cream sandwich to be found. Jack threw his arms up in the air and huffed like a big-shot from LA. "What kind of ice cream place doesn't have ice cream sandwiches!" he bellowed.

Ty, October's Scooper of the Month, wouldn't tolerate Jack's antics and kicked us out. 5:30 Nation piled back into the pickup. Although sandwich-less, we departed the ice cream shop as a unified team on a mission. Our solitary purpose: find ice cream sandwiches!

We tried two local gas station Mini-Marts and ended up with a party-size bag of Cool Ranch Doritos, three packs of beef jerky, and Combos (and gummy peach rings for me, of course), but no ice cream sandwiches. (For fit dudes, these guys sure had an appetite for junk food, which I respected!) Zero for three, we stumbled on the Lone Pine General Store bearing a rustic sign. We hoped—Mark kept encouraging us to manifest it—that *this* was our ice cream sandwich salvation.

Jack, victorious, sprinted to the front with a box of Chipwich Ice Cream Sandwiches, and we waited to tear into them as Jack paid. Vance, a fast-talking lawyer turned Hollywood agent, snagged a mountain map and browsed it as he waited in line to check out.

"Great idea," I said, joining Vance in line with a souvenir map of Mt. Whitney to hang in my basement man cave. Before I could pull up the digital wallet app on my phone to pay, the short, gray-haired, older woman behind the counter grabbed my cell. She lifted her reading glasses up to her eyes, beads dangling around her neck, leaned in close to my phone, and gushed about my girls.

"What a cute picture!" said the cashier. "Grandchildren are so precious, aren't they?"

She handed me the phone. I stared back in utter shock. I looked at the old photo of my daughters cuddled together on a tire swing in the town park.

"When you're our age, you really appreciate those special moments with your grandkids, don't you?"

Vance stepped forward and looked at the woman's name badge. "Hey, Jean, those are his *daughters*."

I angrily stuffed the phone back in my pocket. Jean rang up my Mt. Whitney map, and I paid without saying another word.

My gray hair made me look older than I was, but to be called a grandfather in my mid-thirties was a dagger to the heart. I was speechless, angry, and embarrassed.

I followed the guys outside and Jack tossed me an ice cream sandwich. Vance slapped me on the back and said, "Hey Grandpa—time for your afternoon nap?" I rolled my eyes. "Just busting your balls, Jacob. It's no big deal. That woman was senile."

"What happened?" asked Teddy, armed to make a joke.

Vance explained, "The Elderly Woman Behind the Counter in the Small Town—"

"I love that Pearl Jam song!" Jack interrupted.

"Yeah, great tune. Grandma Jean in there thought Jacob's kids were his grandkids."

The guys erupted in laughter, and when I lowered my head, dejected, I noticed a drop of ice cream on my cargo shorts. Another drop landed on my shirt. *Great*, I thought, *not only is my ego stained, so are my clothes.*

I quietly stewed on the ride back to Mt. Whitney. While the guys were reminiscing about their trip last fall across the Grand Canyon, all I could do was obsess that I'd be turning forty in several years. The thought of that approaching milestone made me quiver, but in my mind, I was not a middle-aged man—my life was just getting started! My kids sometimes teased me about "getting old," but aside from my back seizing up after a long day of running around my office straightening teeth, I felt like I was still in my twenties, although my wife frequently says I *act* like a teenager!

Our trip yielded spoils of ice cream sandwiches and the new nickname "Gramps" for me. It took me back to my playground days at elementary school: picked on for being first out at freeze tag and dubbed "Pokey." I was pissed about that nickname then (I wasn't even as slow as Kenny McFly) just as much as I was pissed about my new nickname thirty years later. "Barlow, tell your boys to stop," I pleaded.

"Dude, it's their way of accepting you into the tribe."

I squabbled back, "Good old Jean just called me a *grandpa*! She aged me up thirty years. Do I really look like a grandpa?"

Teddy, the comedian, overheard my conversation with Barlow and thought it good fodder for a new bit. "Jacob, you don't look that old! I mean, Jean grew up watching TV in black and white, and you grew up watching MTV. She probably still listens to the radio, but you're a Spotify guy. And you're still investing for growth while she's investing for capital preservation!"

5:30 Nation laughed hysterically at Teddy's joke. He continued, "Don't worry about it, bro. My kids are always calling me "Boomer." It's annoying. I mean, I was born in 1970, for Chrissakes! Don't be disrespectful and call me Boomer. Call me X-Man like a comic book superhero! That, I'm okay with!" The members of 5:30 Nation applauded. Teddy bowed, took out a mini spiral notebook, and frantically jotted down his new bit before the words vanished from his memory.

Barlow, seeing the scowl on my face, finally came to my defense. "Fellas, lay off Silverstein, and stop with the Gramps nickname. He doesn't like it. Let him be."

Twenty minutes later, the group filed onto the trail, and I fell in line behind Teddy. I patted his back, acknowledging that I liked his bit. He gave me a thumbs up. During the practice hike, all I could think about were my sore, tired legs and the fact that I was sweating profusely, clearly working harder than any of the Adonises of 5:30 Nation. We weren't even close to the real challenge, and my body was already acting like the seventy-year-old Jean thought I was, and my mind was acting unsettled and immature. But I kept moving, determined to prove that elderly woman behind the counter in a small town wrong.

Chapter 10 – Exposure

Mark strolls over, rocks crunching beneath his boots, causing my flashback to evaporate. I'm brought into the present. "Here we are, top of the switchbacks. I'm proud of you for making it this far, buddy!" I nod slowly, the enormity of what I'd done setting in.

"Hey, look who decided to join us!" Barlow yells from across the trail. We turn our heads, and the other five members of 5:30 Nation appear. So much for our two-hour head start. Like a basketball team coming out of the tunnel for their introductions, the boys sprint towards us with their arms outstretched, and we give them high fives.

They stop and remove their backpacks and hydrate in unison, like well-choreographed synchronized swimmers. Smiles abound as 5:30 Nation basks in our reunion. Sean, a buff personal trainer with a perpetual five o'clock shadow, tells Barlow, "The elevation's tougher than I thought it would be." He checks his vitals on his Garmin watch. "My heart rate's ten beats higher than normal. This climb's for sure harder than the Rim-to-Rim across the Grand Canyon!"

Mumbling through a mouthful of oranges, Sean's younger brother, Casey, says, "Definitely harder than the Grand Canyon." Jack, ever the contrarian, tells the group he'll defer his opinion until he finishes the entire hike.

Teddy agrees with Sean that the altitude makes this hike harder and asks me how I'm feeling.

Smirking, and trying to not sound too excited that I'm fitting in with these fit Californian dudes, I answer, "It's been challenging, but I'm enjoying the journey!"

Casey and Vance finish taking selfies, and the five fast hikers huddle up in front of the Trail Crest Sign. Barlow joins them and waves Mark and me over.

"How much longer until we summit?" I ask, and realize I sound like a kid hounding their parents with, "Are we there yet?"

"About two more miles 'til the top," Mark says.

We sidle up next to Barlow and take our places in the group huddle. Like Ted Lasso before an AFC Richmond Premiere League game, Barlow takes the lead: "Fellas, we're kicking some ass on this mountain! Let's keep pushing ourselves and make sure we get to the summit! Hands in." I stack my hand atop Mark's bear paw and chant with the others: "One…two…three…5:30 Nation!" High fives fly like we've just won the Super Bowl. Am I hanging with the cool kids now? I think so!

"Let's go!" Barlow claps, beckoning the group to move out. "No time to waste—we've gotta keep going."

My lungs burn with every breath at the increased altitude. I muster energy from the group rendezvous and psych myself up to prepare for the peril ahead. Like soldiers marching, we fall in line behind Mark. He yells, "All right, gentlemen! Get ready for the *exposed* part of the trail."

Little did I know that by "exposed part" he meant, "You could die if you slip."

My gait starts to slow when I notice we're approaching a section of the trail connecting two peaks. It's like a bridge crossing without side-rails or barriers to safeguard from a tragic fall. The switchbacks had one side of the mountain to lean on and stabilize yourself against, but all security's lost on this narrow path. I'm bilaterally vulnerable (I just made that hiking term up) with nothing to break my fall but the jagged rocks below.

Mark moves seamlessly along the edge, starting to put some distance between us. When I feel Barlow tailgating me, I make a conscious effort to quicken my pace. "Nice,

Silverstein, you're moving well," Barlow says, encouraging me.

I don't respond. It's taking everything I have to concentrate on making my way through this dangerous terrain. I'm not going to be the one to hold 5:30 Nation back—this time will be different than in high school.

It's the first day of freshman basketball practice. Coach Kitman, a short accounting teacher with a large beer gut, says, "We're only as strong as our weakest link! If each of you boys pull your weight, we'll have a successful season. Suicides! Everyone, line up."

My lungs burn in the cold of the gym, my shin splints shoot bolts of pain through my legs, and my feet pound the gym floor as I run the suicides (a name they probably don't use during these politically correct times, but it appropriately described what you felt like doing after running back and forth across the lacquered hardwood floor of the basketball court a dozen or so times).

Coach Kitman is tough, but initially, I enjoy playing for him. He even seems to appreciate my dedication, though I lack skills and natural talent. I work hard to avoid being the weakest link.

After winning our first five games, the team vibes are sky high. I'm making positive plays every time I come off the bench. It's smooth sailing. Until...

We finish practice with a scrimmage, and I have an atypical case of the dropsies. I might as well have olive oil on my hands. I can't hold on to the ball to save my life. The whistle blares and Coach K drags me by the collar to the back wall of the gym. (He's unusually strong for an accounting teacher.) He repeats his mantra to me, "We're only as good as our weakest link." *Coach K then bellows to the team,* "We'll resume practice when our weak link here learns how to catch the ball." *The whole team watches as he heaves basketballs at me—dodgeball style. After dropping over twenty balls, I finally catch one on bloodied knuckles. I look around with watery eyes and can't find an ally in the world. No one will even look at me. When Coach demands fifty fingertip push-ups from the entire team, he's just being plain cruel. Everyone curses me under their breath but no one more harshly than myself:* youareaterribleteammateyousuck, *I rage in my head.*

Steve Dash, the backup guard, yells, "Move your ass, Weakling!" *and as my high school luck would have it, the nickname sticks. My grades slip, and I start to dread basketball. I tell my parents about my new name, and they take matters into their own hands and talk to their friend whose son is the team captain. The name calling stops, and the team remains undefeated, but I don't. I feel dejected, alone, and I now hate basketball. I feel like I'll never shake the burn off my cheeks, the oozing of my bloody fingers, and the sting of being dubbed* Weakling. *My inner child is wounded forever.*

Freshmen year woes, be damned! I think. If I can stop fixating on past issues, maybe I won't plummet to an untimely death. I'm grateful for survival mode kicking in. I'm grateful for my heightened awareness. I'm grateful for every step I take that doesn't result in a fifty story fall off a cliff. Losing focus now would literally be the end of me and my inner child.

I go slow and steady, concentrating on my breathing like a yogi and using my hiking poles to anchor my wobbly legs. This exposed part of the path is sucking the newfound energy right out of me, like a balloon emptying out with fury. I force myself to stay focused and look straight ahead—I concentrate only on the gritty, messy soil and my brown hiking boots with their black checkered laces, ignoring the expanse around me.

Mark turns around and yells, "Only five more minutes, and we'll be through the exposed trail, buddy."

I'll live. (Probably.)

I'm exhilarated!

Chapter 11 – Strong Feelings

I trudge along, head down, eyes fixated on the blocks of uneven stones along the trail. Whitney is unrelenting and unforgiving. I don't stop to appreciate the expanse of the mountain range, let alone track the man-made miniature rock cairns marking the path. Instead, I focus on my steps so I don't trip and fall headfirst into the abyss below.

"Keep moving, Jacob. We've got a long way to go!" The call rouses me, and "Road to Nowhere" by the Talking Heads pops into my head. I just want to feel like we're getting closer to the summit.

Barlow's deep, booming voice interrupts the song and sends shockwaves through my eardrums. "Wow, check this shit OUT, Silverstein!"

I gaze ahead and see the thin, treacherous path finally opening like the top of a funnel. An end to the exposed terror trail.

"No, look up!" I catch a glimpse of what prompted Barlow's glee. Two majestic birds soar across the horizon against the backdrop of the granite mountain. The red-shouldered hawks are imposing and free. Their brown-and-white checkered wings enable the birds to coast with ease. They circle above. While Barlow admires these magnificent creatures for their beauty, I admire how smart they are, already planning for their next meal; one misstep, and I'm certain to be their dinner. My eyes are drawn to their white-banded tails, but I start to feel dizzy watching the birds' circuitous path. I force my attention back to the trail before I pass out. I know Mother Nature and the hawks' call beckon me to a place of peace, but I'm back to the slog and struggle of the hike.

Mark's waiting for us at the end of the exposed trail. "Drink," he demands.

"Not thirsty," I tell him.

"Yeah, I know. You lose your appetite at high altitudes, but you've gotta drink, Jacob. I mean it." I nod. At this point in my journey, 'In Mark I Trust' has become my mantra. I unscrew the top of my neon green Nalgene bottle and take a swig.

Just as Mark leaves to police the water intake of the other bros, Barlow meanders next to me, eating a bag of peanuts.

Like a magician, another pack of peanuts appears in his hand, and he thrusts it towards me. I ignore him and take another swig of water.

"Sorry I upset you before the switchbacks," he says. "Mark filled me in on why what I said triggered you. That must have been tough." He pauses. I hear the screech of the hawks above our heads.

I haven't seen Andy Barlow show sentimentality since I've known him, but I'm touched by my old friend's sincerity. I grab the peanuts from his outstretched hand, his olive branch. "Thanks."

"You're conquering those past demons! That's what this trip is all about." He punches me in the arm. That's more like the bro-ish Barlow I know.

I tear into the peanut wrapper with my canines. Barlow looks at me incredulously, "Dude, you're an orthodontist." He points to his recently bleached maxillary central incisors. "Teeth, not tools!"

I grumble at Barlow through a mouthful of half-chewed peanuts. "You're right. I do know better, but today I'm a man living on the edge!" I look down at my scuffed boots, "Man, what have you gotten me into?"

"Come on, you're having a good time, Silverstein. Look at that shit-eating grin."

"I'm smiling?" I ask.

"Yeah, you're glowing, dude. Sounds corny, especially coming from me, but you have to admit it's been a blast!"

I feel the smile on my face grow wider. "That's one way to put it."

"Honestly, I'm stoked you're here to share it with me." This is as sentimental as Barlow will get, and I'm touched by his words. I look down. "Dude, are you blushing?" he asks me.

"No! It's just windburn," I blurt. I stuff the peanut wrapper in my backpack and respond with a sappy statement in kind. "It's been awesome reconnecting with you too. You were my inspiration behind this whole excursion. I admire your adventurous spirit. I just want to be as cool as you!"

"We both know that'll never happen." He pauses for my laugh, then continues, "But you've held your own." Barlow stretches out his right arm and opens his palm. I instinctively know what to do. I quickly grasp his right hand, and in a choreographed move that dudes have been doing for generations, we extend our left arms for a bro hug. Our bond is doubly solidified at 13,000 feet.

Barlow laughs spontaneously. "I know it's been hard on you, but you're killing this hike. The guys are all talking about how impressed they are with you!"

"Are you joshing me?" I say, then realize how lame that sounds. I mean, who says "joshing" nowadays? It's like I was transported back to a *Happy Days* episode. Before I can correct myself, Jack, the Iron Man triathlete/investment banker, struts over, and like two male lions in a pride, Barlow and I immediately turn our attention to the alpha male.

"How you feeling, Strong?" Barlow asks Jack.

"Is that your nickname?"

"No, my last name," Jack answers.

"Of course it is," I whisper under my breath and Barlow laughs.

"All good, boys! What a beautiful day, right?" Jack removes his jacket, biceps bulging through his tight polyester Patagonia shirt.

"Yo, Jack, now that I have you alone…" Barlow begins.

I bow my head sheepishly. *What am I, chopped liver?*

Barlow reads my mind. "No offense, Silverstein. It's just that when I'm with Jack, everyone else from 5:30 Nation is around. Anyway, I wanted to ask how you're doing since the divorce? That went down so quickly. Amy and I were shocked. You doin' okay?"

The muscle man appears vulnerable for the first time since I met him. He puts his hands through his thick hair. "I'm not gonna lie, it's been rough. A lot harder than my first divorce. It's a lonely feeling. And having kids really fucking complicates things!"

"I bet." Barlow shakes his head. "Sorry, dude. Was it sudden or did you know it was coming?"

"Sudden," Jack answers curtly.

"I don't think he wants to talk about it," I whisper to Barlow.

Barlow presses on anyway. "I don't mean to pry, but I've always been fascinated with the anatomy of a divorce. I often wonder what leads to the breaking point. Like how much is too much before you call it quits."

"Why? You and Amy getting a divorce too?" Jack asks. "Be careful, it's an epidemic. Spreading like California wildfires. Four of my buddies from high school got divorced last year."

"No, we're good. But Amy thinks every divorce is caused by either financial woes or when the guy cheats. Obviously financial woes weren't the problem…."

"Barlow!" I scold my friend, "It's none of your business."

Jack shrugs. "It's okay, Jacob." He points at Barlow who's eagerly awaiting the answer. "Tell Amy she's wrong."

Barlow snaps his fingers. "I knew it! It's not always the man's fault. But in your case, I wouldn't have been surprised. The ladies are always fawning all over you!"

"It wasn't me who fucking cheated."

"No! Dude, what happened?" Barlow pries.

"Barlow, you're shameless. Stop," I admonish.

Jack, oblivious to our side-conversation continues. "I was working my ass off at the firm. You don't make six figure bonuses slacking off. I was waking up early to take care of our East Coast clients and traveling to meet new investors. Jen wasn't complaining when she got the new Lexus, a vacation home in Reno, or when she was redecorating rooms every month with a carte-blanche budget."

Barlow whispers to me, "Kiss those houses goodbye."

Barlow builds the story like my favorite amateur TV detective—Sean, on *Psych*. "I bet she was upset you weren't home enough. It's like how Amy wants the lifestyle my salary affords us and the comfort it brings but then gets pissed if I'm late for dinner. I gotta ask, though, you weren't getting any side action on your East Coast travels?"

I stare daggers at my dental friend then say, "Barlow, what's gotten into you?"

"Nope," Jack says. "My therapist told me that men cheat when they're not getting enough at home. I was working too hard to even care about that. Women cheat when they're not feeling emotional connection. And if I'm being honest with myself—and after all the money I've paid for therapy, that's the least I can be—I wasn't emotionally present enough for her. So, yeah, Jen's the one who had the affair. But I feel guilty in some ways too."

Barlow shakes his head and takes a deep breath. "Damn, life can be cruel."

"Yeah. She was banging someone from work. And the worst part: it was one of the twins who squealed on her. She'd hide her phone from Luke when he'd try to see who was texting her. My *ten-year-old* tells me this. It's enough to break your heart." Tears are now running down Jack's face. "I still wanted to make it work, but she'd checked out."

"I'm sorry, man. That really sucks." Barlow goes in and embraces Jack in a more-than-bro-hug. It's a full on compassionate, you-can-cry-on-my-shoulder hug. Jack breaks down in Barlow's arms.

I feel like a voyeur, so I distract myself with my phone. I swipe through pictures of Leah and the girls. I miss them. I kick myself for voluntarily leaving them behind for a week. I kick myself for not realizing that Leah *has* been lacking emotional connection from me lately. I'd be devastated if she decided to sow her wild oats with another man and drop my ass in a divorce. I take no joy in Jack's woes, but his tragic situation definitely gives me a fresh perspective.

At the end of the workday, I'm spent. I just want to sit on the couch and scroll through my Facebook feeds for half an hour with an orange soda (I've never been a beer guy). But I need to make a more conscious effort to stay engaged with the family when I come home from work and not hibernate in my man cave like a bear at the first sign of the winter frost. My family deserves more than that. God knows I don't want to slip up at home and have our marriage come crashing down like Jack Strong's.

This tragic thought brings me back to the present because, first things first, I need to make sure I don't slip off the trail and end up as dinner for the circling hungry hawks.

Chapter 12 – Rants and Raves

Mark marches over to us, the 5:30 Nation ants marching behind. Jack and Barlow release their hug. "Let's get ready to rock scramble, boys!"

"Rock scramble? Is there no top to this mountain?" My tone is that of a disbelieving nephew listening to his crazy uncle talk about his UFO abduction. "What's a rock scramble?"

"There's no clear path anymore," Mark explains, "so we hike along those rocks ahead."

"You mean those boulders over there?" I ask in a voice that cracks like William Hung belting out a song on *American Idol*. I feel like I'm lost in a house of mirrors; just when I think I've found my way through the maze, I run smack into another silvered pane of glass. Except when I reach the exit, there's no fun carnival with funnel cake, cotton candy, or my loving family waiting for me.

Barlow interrupts my thoughts, "Put away the hiking poles. You're going to need your hands for balance."

"No one told me about this part," I say.

Barlow's not listening because he's now in front of me leading the way. I reluctantly follow. He turns around, "Let's go. Watch how I navigate through the boulders. Be careful; one misstep can be dangerous. Ready, Jacob?"

Jacob? Oh damn. Whenever Barlow uses my first name, he means business. The last time he called me Jacob, a difficult patient of his was moving from Newport Beach to Matingly, Connecticut, and he asked me to take over her case. What he didn't tell me was that she would be the highest maintenance patient I'd ever treat. She'd call me on the weekends complaining of TMJ pain, and when I didn't call her back *immediately*, she'd complain that I was neglecting her.

"I'm coming, *Andy*," I yell, showing him I'm just as serious about this part of the hike as he is.

The organized, tight conga-line formation we previously had is now fraying. Like mountain goats, the five fast hikers from 5:30 Nation have no problem traversing the rocks. They're fifty-plus feet ahead of Barlow and me. Mark is ahead of us but behind the alpha males, intentionally holding back so we stay within his sight.

"You good?" Barlow turns back and asks. I give him a shrug. Without hiking poles, I'm doing everything I can to get balance as I straddle over two super-sized rocks. My hands grab the cold and jagged boulders to steady myself. Barlow starts to pull away from me, and I hear him say from a distance, "I'm going to catch up with the dudes." He effortlessly jumps to the next rock. Why am I surprised by his agility?

He makes quick work of crossing the high-angled rocks, passing Mark and leaving me in the dust. Barlow, my best buddy, the one who encouraged me to take this journey in the first place and who spent countless hours on the phone with me philosophizing about how meaningful summiting the mountain together would be, deserts me at this pivotal moment. He and the rest of 5:30 Nation are nearly out of sight. But should I expect them to dampen their own experience just to make sure I'm okay?

It's been thirty minutes on the rock scramble, and although Mark is a blur on the horizon, he's still in sight. I squint to follow his movements as he glides from rock to rock. I am nowhere near as graceful and find it challenging to keep up with him. He hollers back to me, "Hustle! We're already an hour behind schedule." He wants to reach the summit by 12:30 p.m., but it's already noon, and we still have over an hour to go. I pay less and less attention to him.

I pick up my pace, scrambling as fast as I can. This section is not particularly steep, especially compared to the switchbacks, but the thin air at 13,000 feet is making it hard to breathe. My lungs never feel like they're filled to capacity. The combination of perpetual shortness of breath and not having a sturdy foundation to hike on pummels me.

It feels like crawling through a minefield—if I were to trip on a jagged edge and fall to my left, the open air would certainly not slow my fall. I grip each boulder so tightly my knuckles turn white.

I've lost all feeling in my fingers now, but I don't care. It's about survival. I must keep scrambling. I can't be the one to die on this hike—that would be too embarrassing. I focus all my effort on moving from one boulder to another. With each rock I cross, I approach the summit, but with no end in sight, I'm deflating.

Multi-tones of gray surround me. Not even a bright spot of yellow dandelion pokes through. I drift out of my body, floating somewhere. I imagine this is what the first explorers on the moon felt like.

"Keep going, Silverstein," I say out loud. My mental pep talk picks up. "You can do this! You've got your family to go home to. Leah and the girls need you!" I'm screaming now, not to the NASA station back in Houston, but to myself: "Hold the fuck on!"

I feel like a lunatic, literally shouting at myself on the mountain. But if I let go, I'm dead. Now I wish I had doubled my life insurance for Leah and the girls.

"Mark!" I call out to my adopted guide, but he's no longer within earshot.

I'm frantically trying to catch up, but suddenly, my foot slips, and I fall backwards off a boulder. Pain shoots through my right leg. I look down to see my shin bleeding.

"MARK?" No answer. "BARLOW?" No answer.

I collapse on the granite ledge that just split open my shin and look down at the trickling blood seeping through the thick hair on my leg. Darkness creeps in at the edges of my vision, and I'm a stone statue just like the one I sit on.

I hear the words, *drink water*, and turn to look for the origin of the voice. Through my blurry vision, I see no one.

My tongue is thick and heavy in my mouth, and molten daggers are piercing my throat. I upend my Nalgene bottle, but only a few drops fall into my mouth. I can barely swallow. I drop the empty bottle. Bright flashes strobe in my line of sight, and my heart thuds in my head. There are suddenly hundreds of hawks circling, shrieking and dancing to the rhythm of my throbbing pulse, just waiting until the music stops. It's like a rave. A red-shouldered hawk rave. *Thump. Thump. Thump.* Even the boulders are moving to the beat now.

"We…problem…Houston," I croak.

Chapter 13 – Clown Show

"Hey, are you alright?"

Head down, still unable to move, I can't even shake my head to respond to this faint female voice.

I whisper, "Leah? Leah?"

"No, my name is Allie. You look in bad shape. Take some of my water. Don't try and grab the bottle; your hand is too shaky. Here."

Water cools my cracked lips. Like a baby's instinct to suckle on a breast, I sip from this woman's water bottle.

"Let's go, Allie!" I hear a voice howl. "I'm done taking a leak. Come on."

"Someone needs my help!" she shouts.

"Come on. We're behind schedule. Get moving NOW!"

"I've got to go. Tyler can be a jerk sometimes, but take this," I look down and see a granola bar in my hand. Lifting my eyes up, I catch a glimpse of long, braided, strawberry-red hair. Just like that, she's gone. I nibble on the granola bar.

The kindness of a stranger passing by is enough to revive me. Allie, my guardian angel on the mountain, has restored my faith in humanity. The cold, brisk breeze vaporizes the sweat on my face. I shiver. Cold penetrates my skin and sinks deep into my bones, but I'm too tired to reach into the backpack and add another layer for warmth. The pounding of my heart doesn't even distract me from the chill of the wind barraging my entire body. The deep breathing technique Mark taught me from his stay at a Buddhist monastery in Sri Lanka isn't working. Without realizing I'm speaking, I hear myself say, "Don't panic, Silverstein. Think rationally. WWMD?" *What Would Mark Do?*

A voice inside my head answers, *I told you this was a bad idea! We should have never come on this trip. Forget WWMD! YATF—You Are Totally Fucked!*

A more rational inner-voice retorts, *I should wash your mouth out with soap like Dad used to do when we cursed. Come on, Jacob, things are never as bad as they seem. Let's not ruin our special spiritual journey.*

The doubter, my inner child, responds, *Spiritual journey? More like a spiritual crisis! We're in a scary situation here. Be realistic. It's bad, dude.*

Listening to the inner child, I take stock of my situation:

I'm stranded on the side of a mountain with a bloodied leg. My water bottle is empty. I'm ravenous and delirious with exhaustion. I'm pissed at myself. And I'm afraid. My muscles scream for more oxygen, but no matter how slowly and deeply I breathe, I can't satisfy the demands of my body. I'm shivering uncontrollably. And to top it all off, there's no more Mark to encourage me. No more Barlow to push me. No 5:30 Nation to accompany me up the mountain. Once again, I'm the outsider yearning to fit in, yet I find myself alone.

The inner child reminds me that this has always been the hair shirt I bear: *Remember Bobo?*

"How could I forget." My exhausted mind drifts away to a faded memory of Montessori preschool and the first time I felt like an outcast:

The teacher announces a special guest, and Bobo the Clown appears. He's met by tremendous cheers from my excited classmates, but I withhold my enthusiasm as this stranger with a red nose, white-painted face, and flaming orange hair shuffles into our class. I stare at his canoe-sized shoes and drift off into a daydream only to be startled back to life: A-OO-GAH, A-OO-GAH, A-OO-GAH. Every other four-year-old runs to Bobo as he squeezes his clown horn, but I'm frozen in place. All alone in the back of the class, my brain struggles to process the commotion, and I burst into tears.

The teacher kneels by my side, compassionately whispering in my ear, "It'll be okay, dear. You're safe," and when that doesn't work, she shoves a feather-soft, light-brown teddy bear that smells like vanilla into my arms. I can't catch the lump in my throat and wipe my runny nose with my sleeve, while everyone else watches Bobo. The class laughs uproariously; I continue to sob. Eventually, my mom appears in the doorway. My cheeks burn with tears and shame, covered in snot. Neither a hug from my mom nor the plush teddy pressed against my cheek can calm me down.

Fresh tears, as salty as Barlow's peanuts, stream down my wind- and sunburned cheeks and into my mouth. I'm powerless and small just like when Bobo robbed me of my sense of safety, security, and self in preschool.

And you thought things would be different this time, teases the inner child. Nasty and unapologetic he rants in my head:

Face it. Things just come easier for guys like Barlow and Mark. This whole thing was a pathetic attempt to be one of the cool kids. You're an outsider, a freak. You'll never fit in!

What I need to do next becomes as clear as the white clouds hovering above me. With all the energy I can muster, I grab my backpack and stand up. I ignore the pain in my shin and start descending the mountain.

Chapter 14 – The California Pep Talk

"Dude! What the fuck are you doing?"

I stop and slowly turn around. A familiar figure is rushing toward me. Mark, agile and confident as ever, is suddenly in my face. I wipe the tears from my eyes. "What happened?" he asks.

My voice cracks, barely audible. "I fell. I'm bleeding. I'm totally spent…heading down."

In one fluid motion, he removes his backpack, takes out the first aid kit, and hands me a bag of his homemade trail mix and a bottle of 5-Hour Energy. As I swig down the drink like a shot of tequila, Mark wipes my bloodied shin with gauze and stinging antiseptic.

When he's done bandaging me up, Mark places his hands on my shoulders. I feel my tension draining away. He leans in to talk to my rational self. "Listen, I'm gonna be honest with you. You're a super nice guy, and I've enjoyed getting to know you. But when I saw you start the hike, I thought there was no way this wiry guy from Connecticut was going to make it to the top of the mountain."

I look at Mark with surprise in my eyes. If he's trying to encourage me, he's not doing a great job.

"But here you are, *almost at the summit*," he continues. "We're only an hour to the top—you can totally do this! You're tougher and more determined than you give yourself credit for...than *I* gave you credit for."

I look away. Mark grabs my cheeks, swivels my head towards his face, and looks deep into my eyes. "Trust me—if you turn back now, you'll regret it. We're all so close. The guys are waiting for you. Let's go."

As embarrassed as I was to be this tall, dorky-looking guy left behind by the buff dudes from 5:30 Nation, Mark's California pep talk sets me straight. Unequivocally. His words seep into my soul.

"Come on, brother!" Mark punches me in the shoulder, and it's the giddy-up I need.

Trail mix sugars jolt me with adrenaline; I turn around, and we start ascending Whitney again.

Chapter 15 – Solid Ground

Relief comes with an exhale. I glance back at the trail stretched out behind us and am grateful for the solid granite under our feet after the rock scramble. I dig into my backpack, take out Mark's hiking poles, unfold them, and after spiking them in the dirt, I start moving up the mountain again. My heart works overtime to perfuse organs, but I keep walking. The piercing winds rush past my exposed cheeks.

Mark is by my side. Despite it all, we're making the summit push. I don't know how Mark stays focused at my tortoise pace, but he does.

After twenty minutes of hiking, I break the silence. "Sorry, Mark. I can't take it anymore." The sudden drop in temperature has turned my fingers white. With all the drama on the mountain, I guess I forgot to cover my hands. Fingers cracking, I slip on my thermal gloves.

"Hydrate," Mark reminds me. "We can't let altitude sickness get you now." I force down a few gulps.

"Coming through on your left!" says a sinewy, fit woman in her mid-thirties as she breezes by us. She is followed by three more athletic ladies. They look like yoga moms, determined to summit Mt. Whitney no matter who's in their way.

I grumble and sneer at the people passing me and consider stabbing the next one in the foot with my hiking pole. I sense my snail's crawl drains and irritates Mark; he's ready to roll, and I'm holding him back. Gone are his encouraging pep talks and his endless patience with me. He's all business as we approach the summit.

After another twenty minutes of hiking the monotonous path, we've fallen into the flow of summiteers like a school of fish. When we turn the next corner, I spot a couple clad in red North Face coats, hoods up to shield them from the blistering cold.

As we approach, something about being out in the wilderness on the mountain inspires me to be a good Samaritan. "Do you guys want me to take a picture of you?"

"Do you mind?" asks the man.

"That would be great!" the woman says.

Ignoring Mark's glare, I grab the woman's phone, remove my gloves for a second (despite them, my fingers are now purple), aim, and take their picture. The couple thanks me and tries to make small talk, "How are you enjoying the landscape?"

Before I can answer, Mark beckons, "Jacob, let's go!" He speaks to the couple rashly, "I'm sorry, but my friend and I are *very* behind schedule." I stay quiet and nod, searching for whatever strength is left from my last shot of 5-Hour Energy to keep me moving.

No one from 5:30 Nation is in sight. I fear they arc leagues ahead of us. As we continue along, I'm about to admonish Mark for his rudeness but realize I didn't even have an answer for the couple's question. Was I "enjoying the landscape?" I snap myself out of my hiking trance and decide to check out the scenery. It feels like eons ago that we encountered plush green vegetation and tall pine trees decorating the path. Hours have passed since we crossed creeks trickling over our boots and balanced ourselves along logs. Now I notice that the clear blue sky pops against the gray rocks pile along the mountaintop. What the trail lacks in discernable beauty, it makes up for with sweeping panoramic vistas.

"Mark, do you mind if we stop and check out the view for a minute?"

I expect him to give me a hard time, but he surprisingly agrees to another break. Moving a few steps off the trail, I peer into the valley thousands of feet below. Surprisingly, I don't feel lightheaded or dizzy with vertigo as I look out at the vast horizon. Instead, I admire Mother Nature in all her grandiosity. The expansive scenery engulfs me, and I realize I've been so focused on the destination that I've ignored the beauty of this part of the trek. Shame on me for forgetting the most important lesson of the hike—*enjoy the journey*!

I look around to share my newfound revelation with Mark, but he's nowhere in sight. I shout his name. After my third holler, he responds, "I'll be right there." Following his voice, I cross the trail. "Give me a minute," he says.

I pivot and see Mark ten feet away crouching behind a pile of rocks. He is not concealing himself very well; his bare ass is sticking out. "Uh, Mark, what do you think you're doing?"

"What does it look like I'm doing?"

"Looks to me like you're taking a dump on the mountain," I answer.

"Guess you got into Harvard for more than your good looks and charming personality!"

"That and I slept with the admissions officer," I joke. Getting back to the situation at hand, I ask him, "Don't you think you should have a little more privacy? I can literally see your asshole."

"Hey, when you've gotta go, you've gotta go! Keep walking. I'll catch up."

I turn to get a head start and see the North Face couple approaching. "Yo Mark, that couple I took a picture of is, um, coming towards us. Maybe you want to be a little more concealed."

"Can't move now," he replies.

The woman gives a friendly wave. "Where's your buddy?" the guy asks. Before I can answer, they notice Mark, or at least the back half of him. I half expect them to be like drivers rubbernecking at a horrific accident, but when the couple realizes they are seeing Mark unloose a caboose behind a rock, they rush past and politely say, "Well, good to see you again. Safe travels to the summit!"

I feel so embarrassed for my new friend but decide to let it go. When the couple is well out of sight, I tell him, "I'm impressed you did your business in public. I've never pooped outside before! I can't even pee next to people at a urinal, let alone on the side of a mountain."

"Are you kidding me?"

I look over my shoulder to ensure there's no one around. "I can't believe I'm talking about this out loud. But, yes, I get too self-conscious when I pee in public. I get pee stage fright!"

"That's some deep psychological shit right there, no pun intended! You afraid your wiener's too small or something?"

I look down, totally embarrassed by the turn the conversation has taken. "I have no idea what or who to compare it to. It's probably average. Maybe a little disproportionate for my height, but my wife has never complained!"

Mark laughs, "That's a good one. You should do comedy on the side, like Teddy."

A group of hikers is gaining on us, and I hear, "On your left."

Mark continues, "Here's some advice that will serve you well. Don't waste time caring what people think about you. Fuck them! If they want to judge you, let them. You know the truth, and don't let anyone out there tell you differently. We need to work on your self-confidence!"

He's right. I care way too much about what people think. The group behind us speeds past. I am too self-conscious to tell Mark about the traumatic time I tried to pee in public at

Fenway Park in Boston. The epic fail still seethes in my psyche:

I'm at a Yankees–Red Sox game, rooting for the away team. During the seventh-inning stretch, I rush to the bathroom. The line is ten deep to use the urinals and even longer for the stalls. When it's my turn, I realize I have to pee in the dreaded trough. The trough is the Wild West of urinals. It's like a gigantic gutter coming out of the ground—no barriers, no privacy, pee flying everywhere. I step up to the trough and unzip. A few minutes go by...nothing. The fans in the bathroom start to heckle me. "Oy, 'urry up! I've got to take a wicked pissa! And the Yankees suck!" (They've obviously noticed my Yankees hat.) I'm sweating profusely. Finally, after another three painful minutes, I fake the shake and zip up. I walk away defeated—like the Yankees that day—with a full bladder until I find a family bathroom and relieve myself in private.

"We'll address your urination problems another day, dude." Mark punches me in the arm. I close my eyes and wince in pain to myself. "Look up there! You can make out the hut on top of the summit! We're just minutes away, Jacob!"

I smile. I commit to full physical and mental presence on this last leg of the journey. *Stay in the moment*, I coach myself. *Leave everything else behind.* So what if I can't pee in public, while Mark here uses the side of a mountain as his personal latrine. Instead of feeling jealous of my new friend, I choose to appreciate and admire the freedom he embodies. The freedom of being on this glorious mountaintop.

Chapter 16 – Peak Perfect

Mark turns around, points, and bellows, "Keeler Needle and Crooks Peak! We're at the end, my friend!"

Pan the camera in for a close-up! The relief on my face is visible. The summit is minutes away. Exhaustion quickly converts to exhilaration when I spot the sturdy, old, gray stone hut with a corrugated aluminum roof. The famous marker on top of Mt. Whitney leans forward, beckoning me towards the summit.

Surprisingly, I do not rush to the pinnacle. Instead, my stomach sinks, and my brain spins wildly out of control, wondering if the reality of summiting will measure up to what I've been anticipating for all these months. My wounded inner child attempts to crush my moment of exhilaration and bliss: *The nirvana you've been seeking won't be at the top of this mountain! I'd stop here before you're disappointed— like all the other times in your life.*

"Stop it," I implore the inner voice. There's no time for childhood flashbacks now. Still, the nagging worry that the pinnacle won't live up to my expectations rests somewhere on my shoulders. Will the real moment live up to what I'd imagined?

Howling wind whips across the mountain top. Swirling dust slaps my face, which is enough to silence my inner child. I even appreciate that dust right now—maybe it's Mother Nature's way of patting me on the back. I shuffle over the flat granite stones that cover Whitney's top. Before I spot any of the 5:30 Nation, I join a group of people lined up as if they're looking out onto the Atlantic Ocean off of Provincetown, Massachusetts, searching for whales. My sapped legs realize there's nowhere else to go.

I've reached the end of the trail.

It

Does

Not

Disappoint!

I've summited Mt. Whitney!

I hunch over, breathless, but not because of the altitude. The sublime panoramic vantage point from the peak leaves me stunned, gasping for air. I bow my head in a mix of overwhelming and reverential respect for the mountain. I say a silent prayer, thanking Whitney for allowing me to reach her summit and sending all my love and gratitude to my amazing wife and daughters for their sacrifices while I embarked on this journey.

I right myself and take in the grand scenery; I let the beauty of each frame freeze in my mind. I stand above a line of cotton-like clouds clumped together at the edge of the horizon. I gaze in awe of the vastness of the valleys below and the boundless sky above. I'm floating in heaven! I feel a million feet tall—like I could pluck the miniature trees below and scoop up the mountain ridges in the distance.

All the people scattered about on top of the world form our own small-but-mighty community atop Mt. Whitney. I make eye contact and smile at the yoga moms, who are using a flat boulder for a tabletop as they eat their brie and Trader Joe's crisps. They flash their beautifully bleached, straight teeth at me and then provide a thumbs up, confirming we're all in this together. A couple next to me speaks in French, and although I can't understand them, I feel their excitement and relief in having summited. No translator needed: they speak my language by holding up their hands, and we high five—our shared understanding that this moment is monumental. We've bonded with Mother Nature, the summit, and one another. We'll remember this for the rest of our lives.

I step away from the crowd, remove my backpack, and lay across a large rock tablet the size of the Ten Commandments. With no clouds to block the sun, its radiant rays intensely brighten the landscape and bathe my skin. Like a Jew for Jesus, I stretch out my arms in a cross, symbolically calling to the Universe. *I'm home.*

A sense of total peace and understanding engulfs me. My mind floats over my body like a helium balloon, and I embrace the detachment. This moment means everything. I never want it to end. Alone, immersed in the natural landscape and the accomplishment of it all, tears stream down my cheeks. They're tears of sadness because I know I'll never have this feeling of euphoria again, no matter how much I try. I want this love to last forever. *The Universe and I are one.*

"Silverstein!"

I open my eyes, and Barlow is standing above me like a priest baptizing a baby. And with that, Wordsworth's "spot of time" in my life vanishes. Perhaps forever.

I stand up and we embrace like long lost relatives, not letting go of our gigantic bear hug. Mark comes over and joins us. "We did it! I'm so proud of you, Jacob!"

I put my arms around Barlow and Mark, and like the three amigos, we stare out at the horizon.

"Fucking amazing!" Barlow keeps repeating.

Jack comes over and massages my shoulders.

Teddy rubs my head, and Vance slaps me on the back, "You're here, brother!"

Sean and his real brother, Casey, rush up and give me high fives.

The eight of us huddle up. There are no bro hugs when you get to 14,505 feet above sea level. It's a full-on hug fest from everyone in 5:30 Nation!

Out of the corner of my eye, I catch a fit, elderly man in his sixties and ask if he would mind taking a picture of us. Without saying a word, he pats me on the back and takes my cell. The guys gather, and on the count of three, this moment becomes frozen in time, a memory to cherish forever. The man gives my phone back to me, and I look at the photo. My grin is as broad as Niagara Falls. I am euphoric. It's perfect for posting on Instagram for Cole and my gym rat bros back in Connecticut! All I need now is cell service.

The hot sun beats down on my face. I peel my jacket off as I sit on a round, flat boulder, looking like the Arthurian table of legend, perched next to Barlow. Although my entire body hurts like I just finished running the Boston Marathon, I feel amazing and ignore my aches and pains. Like pregnancy amnesia, I have forgotten all the stress it took to get here. This baby was worth the struggle. Barlow and I stare out at the vast horizon on the craggy summit.

As we sit in silence, I feel my doubting, skeptical inner child sidle up next to me. I smile at him. *I told you we could do this! We've overcome hard times in the past, and as long as we believe in ourselves, we can do anything.*

My inner child is quiet, reflective, maybe subtly healing and letting go.

Rational-minded, big-brother me harkens my inner child back to when I was on the Middletown Musketeers high school basketball team. I shudder back to the memory of when the coach stopped practice after I kept dropping passes. I remind my doubting self that we left out an important part of that flashback: despite being given the nickname "Weakling," I vowed I would not hold the team back. I did fingertip pushups each night to strengthen my grip, making sure I would never drop a pass again. Even with decreased playing time, I never stopped showing up (even if I threatened to in my head). Not only was I part of a conference-winning team, but I was also awarded the Musketeer Medal by Coach K, which was given to "a team player who overcomes adversity and displays the work-ethic, perseverance, and dedication it takes to be a winner." I still have the medal in my memory box along with old love letters from Leah and ticket stubs from concerts and sporting events.

"Dude, let's refuel. Here's a sandwich."

I forgot that Barlow packed our lunches. Seeing the processed deli meat from the Lone Pine General Store incites my ravenous appetite. The first bite of the ham and cheese sandwich causes my empty stomach to jump for joy. For good measure, Barlow hands me his bag of potato chips, and the crunch of the ruffled ridges in my mouth are a perfect complement.

With half my sandwich remaining, Mark walks up to Barlow and me. "Let's go, boys. Time to begin our descent."

"Already?" I ask.

"Yeah, dude." Mark claps his hands for emphasis. "Need I remind you we got here later than planned? We need to get down before it gets too dark."

I take another bite of my sandwich, and Mark senses my reluctance to get up. "Jacob, I'm not playing. We've got to head down!"

Barlow takes off his outer jacket shell and stuffs it in his backpack. He pops up from his squat and puts on his pack. I grab Barlow's outstretched hand, and he yanks me up from my abbreviated picnic on the summit. Jack is leading the alpha male section of 5:30 Nation off the summit, and I quickly stuff my half-eaten lunch into my backpack and join the fellas as Mark pushes me ahead. We pass a sign that says, "Congratulations, you have reached the summit of Mt. Whitney, but you're only halfway home!" My stomach churns a little, from hunger or queasiness I'm not sure.

It's time to retrace my steps.

Chapter 17 – Descent

...but you're only halfway home!

Normally I'm not a vulgar guy, but my first thought after reading the sign is, *are you fucking kidding me?* I risked life and limb to get up this mountain, damn near killing myself, not to mention all the family time I sacrificed, and my hike is only halfway done. I give the summit's public service announcement a mental middle finger.

I pass the Hut and fall in line with 5:30 Nation. Like Army troopers who have parachuted onto the summit on a special ops mission, we snake our way down the mountain. Unlike our bifurcated ascent, we're one big happy tribe hiking in unison. The group is full of ecstasy (the emotion, not the drug), and like school kids on the first day of class talking incessantly about their summer, the boys share trials and tribulations from their ascent. I am reminded of when I was in college, working out (trying to get buff for the ladies!), and the basketball players took a liking to me. They appreciated my max effort in the gym and even asked me to be their team manager. I didn't have time, but their acceptance of me as one of their own always stuck with me. Now, for another moment in time, I have the chops to hang! Like at the college gym, I relish being one of the guys. I keep pace with The Fab Five: Jack, Teddy, Sean, Casey, and Vance. Even though I'm happy to be part of the crew, albeit short-lived, I'm reluctant to share my experience on the mountain for fear of showing more weakness. I choose to listen and soak in everyone's highs and lows from the hike: Adonis Jack's hands shook as he crossed the exposed part of the trail. Teddy, the dermatologist/comedian, lost his comedy notebook along the trail. Vance had to stop to pee every thirty minutes, a side-effect of the Diamox he took to prevent altitude sickness. Sean had trouble breathing because of his asthma, and if not for his nebulizer, he would have turned back and descended the mountain with his brother, Casey. I puff my chest out a little knowing that, just like me, each of these rough and tough guys had their own personal struggles during the journey.

…but you're only halfway home! The words continue to echo through my mind when we hit the rock scramble. Making it to

the summit took everything I had. When Mark beckoned me to head down the mountain, I didn't think I had anything left in the tank. After forcing myself to spring to my feet, the endorphin high from reaching the summit dissipated my exhaustion and bitterness of having to descend the mountain. There was no longer a desire to stop for a snack or to hydrate: all eyes were on returning home now. The path propels me down as if to say, "I've enjoyed you as a guest at my home, but don't let the door hit you in the ass on the way out!" The mountain does not make the journey easy. The rock scramble on the way down is just as brutal as it was on the way up. One wrong step on a boulder and I could break my ankle, leaving me unable to get back to sea level in 206 pieces.

We traverse a narrow pass overlooking a straight vertical drop to death, and I catch the end of a conversation between Teddy and Barlow.

I turn to them, dismayed. "Wait…WHAT logbook?"

Teddy responds that there was a logbook outside the Hut. "You know, where you sign your name to document you summited the mountain."

I think he's joking (that's the problem with comedians, you never know if they're serious). He tells me, "Bro, I'm *dead serious.* All the guys signed it. Our names are etched in immortality—summiteers of Mt. Whitney." My heart sinks.

Not only did I *not* notice a logbook, no one in 5:30 Nation had bothered to clue me in, and now, after a nine-hour, grueling hike, there's no documentation that I was even on Mt. Whitney. My name will never be in the logbook. I look over at Barlow who shrugs as if to say, "That sucks!"

I stew in my own thoughts. *What the hell? Why didn't anyone tell me?* The adrenaline high helping me get down the mountain is gone. Left out, *again*. I slump my shoulders. The thrill of being with the boys is lost, and I'm back to the familiar feeling of being ostracized. My mind flashes back to when I was in college, and I desperately wanted to join a fraternity. Being a late bloomer, I decided to rush Alpha Beta my sophomore year, the fraternity that my buddies all pledged as freshman. My friends were eager for me to join their tribe, so it felt like a slam dunk—I was going to become a brother! Bid night arrived, and I anxiously awaited my invitation. I grew excited when the group rustled outside my dorm room. All the commotion soon passed, and when I peeked my head into the empty hallway, there was a deafening silence. There was no bid for me, but my euphoric neighbor, Aaron, was holding his bid with shaky hands. I spent the rest of the night sobbing, face down in my bed, rejected and dejected. My buddies from Alpha Beta came back to my room later that night, sat down next to me while I buried myself in my damp pillow, and apologetically explained that one of the upperclassmen thought I was "annoying" (apparently, I was in his math class and asked too many questions), and he'd blackballed me. I was excluded from the frat's Bid Day—their version of a summit logbook. Different time, different place, same result. *On the outside looking in.*

My hand slips on a rock. I slice open my palm and stumble backwards, jolted from my wallowing daydream. Mark—ever my guardian angel—catches me. He wipes the cut with antibiotic ointment and places a Band-Aid over it, and my mountain monk finds the right words:

"I heard you didn't sign the logbook." These guys gossip more than my wife's friends at Mahjong.

I nod.

"I know you're frustrated, but remember, we *all* made it to the summit! You don't need your name in a book to prove what you did. It's in here." He pounds his chest with his fist. "You're one of us, and you showed everyone what a big heart you have!"

He's right. I let go of my anger and direct my focus on getting off this rock scramble. The journal of my journey will bear witness to my summit. But, if you, Dear Reader, ever ascend to the top of Mount Whitney, feel free to pen my name in the logbook with the date: 10/12/2012.

...but you're only halfway home! The quote is becoming my mantra during the descent. We're at the ninety-seven switchbacks, and I harken back to my fear and anxiety of climbing this section five hours ago. I head down the switchbacks a different man. No longer feeling the pressure of having to reach the summit by a certain time, I immerse myself in the surroundings. Funny how time changes one's perspective. Instead of dreading the switchbacks, I now appreciate the ingenuity of using them to ascend such a steep elevation without having to rely on mountaineering. And thank heavens for the hiking poles that Mark lent me. They bear the impact of my knees pounding against the granite trail. Gravity ushers me down the mountain faster than I anticipate. We come across a cabled section, and the twined metal is cold against my palms. I hold on tight, so I don't slip on the snowy path.

I turn to Mark, "Where did these cables come from?"

Mark laughs. "Really? You don't remember holding onto them for dear life on the way up?"

I stare blankly at him and shake my head. My cheeks burn. I have no memory of the cables.

He continues, "It's always icy or snowy on this part of the switchbacks. The cables are here so hikers don't slide off the side of the mountain."

As I make my way across stones that have been integrated into the trail, I look above me one more time, trying to rouse a memory of the cables. Do I have amnesia? I bang my head with my gloved hand, trying to dislodge the memory. Still nothing. I grab my hiking pole, dig it into the dirt and, as gravity propels me down the switchbacks, I grit my teeth in disbelief that I still can't recall crossing this section of the trail on the way up.

Mark looks at me concerned, "You okay, dude? I'm worried about you."

I stand more upright, and this time, I'm the one reassuring Mark. "Yeah, I'm good. I must have been so focused on ascending the switchbacks that details got lost along the way. But now, I'm going to stay present and let the scenery set in my mind."

Mark nods. We continue to hike down the switchback in silence. I enjoy every step of the way.

...but you're only halfway home! I'm at the Trail Camp, *way more* than halfway to the trail head, our final destination. I'm still hiking next to Mark as Barlow shoots the shit with the

alpha males. We stop for a water break, and, out of habit, I pull out my phone and check for a text from Leah and my girls.

Mark looks at me and laughs. "It's funny how addicted we are to our phones, isn't it?" I admit to him that I've found it refreshing to unplug for a day. Mark tells me I should try doing what he does: become a Luddite each weekend. After my puzzled look, he explains that a Luddite is a person who dislikes technology and disconnects from all electronics to free their mind of distractions. I admire him for committing to an electronic-free existence each weekend, but I have questions.

"What about your family? Don't you need to stay connected to them?" I ask.

Mark cannot stop laughing at my question.

"What's so funny?"

"Oh, I'm connected to them. Sometimes *too* connected. When I come home from work and see that the Sequoia is not in the garage, I'm the happiest guy on the planet! I love my alone time!"

I ask if he's being real.

"Oh, yes! When no one is around, I'm in heaven. It's so peaceful having the house to myself."

"That surprises me. You sound like a different Mark. I thought you'd be all about your family, all the time! I mean, I miss my family so much since I've been away. It's been weird not hearing from Leah and the kids while I've been on the mountain."

"Don't get me wrong, Jacob, I'm a great dad and husband, but all the noise and drama at home drives me nuts sometimes! The kids and my wife make such a mess—I can't stand it. I organize the house and clean up after those slobs *all* the time. I love a neat house along with my solitude."

This innocent little conversation astonishes me. I cannot believe what I'm hearing from my mountain spiritual guru. He's been caring and thoughtful on the hike—wanting to see everyone succeed and giving so much of himself—it never dawned on me that he would sacrifice family time to be reclusive. It's like a punch in the gut to hear Mark talk so callously about his family. I'm disappointed to see behind the veil and hear about his family frustrations. It's like when your childhood hero refuses to give you an autograph; it's crushing to realize they're a jerk. But part of me finds it reassuring to know my hiking idol is human and has personal issues just like the rest of us. Mother Nature's truth serum leaves me appreciating his raw honesty, and I find comfort in hearing about his Achilles heel.

...but you're only halfway home! The quote should be vanquished from my head by now since there's less than an hour until we're back at base camp. Darkness descends along the trail, and the five triathletes in our group have out-paced us. *Deja vu.* Just like at the 3:00 a.m. start, we've broken off into two groups. Barlow, Mark, and I put our dorklights on so we can inch closer to the trail head with our path illuminated. Conversation is scarce and our breathing is labored. We descend the mountain with a singular mission: to make it down as fast as we can to join the Fab Five for dinner. With a half hour to go, I'm part of the 5:30 Nation diaspora, each of us going at our own pace, in our own world, yet still entrenched in the Mt. Whitney community. There's no reason for the fellas to wait up for me since I'm on autopilot as I head down, down, down. To distract myself from the drudgery of these last miles, I plug my phone into headphones and listen to music. *My Rockin' Hiking Mix* is the perfect complement to the movie trailer in my mind replaying the highs and lows of the trek up Mt. Whitney. I sing along to Pearl Jam, Blink-182, and The Killers with no inhibition. Despite being tone deaf, I shout the lyrics out loud, and people stare at me like I'm a crazy person walking through the subway of New York City.

Although the tribe's dispersed (the Fab Five are surely already at the pub by now), I am feeling at one, in spirit, with 5:30 Nation. I laugh, thinking back to the logbook fiasco. *With enough time and perspective, everything works out!* It's like how, after not getting that invitation to join Alpha Beta, I picked myself up and ran for class president...and won! That decision turned out to be life-changing. In student government, I found a community of my own and developed confidence and communication skills. Most importantly, I forged a relationship with the Dean of Students, Donald Albertsen—a charismatic and engaging father-figure, while we worked on a ceremony for Dean's List students that was my brainchild. He wrote an amazing recommendation letter for me that, I'm convinced, helped me get into Harvard School of Dental Medicine. There you have it—with each setback in life, be it with family, friends, bosses, or even a hike up the highest mountain in the contiguous United States, when you keep your eyes open, a shining light can appear, no matter the adversity!

...You're home! Exhausted, I step off the rocky path. Mark and Barlow await my arrival at the trail head sign. I muster up the last bit of energy that remains, and I rush up to them. We high five and hug it out. A sense of calm and peace

overcomes me. I open my gaze to the sky, and my heart to Mt. Whitney's trail—to new possibilities—and bask in the comfort of knowing that whatever comes next, I'll be ready. The mountain has prepared me for the next steps, the next challenges, the next layers of my life.

Chapter 18 – Fraternity

I enter the Lone Pub and rush to the bathroom to wash my hands now that I'm back in civilization. There are no paper towels, and the hand drier is broken, so I stride with damp hands to the long table where the Fab Five are already three drinks in. Fried appetizers are scattered across their plates. (There's no such thing as being health conscious after a twenty-two-mile, round-trip hike to an elevation of over 14,000 feet.) Barlow and Mark have already seated themselves in the middle, and I take the last spot at the head of the table. I feel like Norm entering *Cheers* when the seven members of 5:30 Nation yell, "Silverstein!"

Adonis Jack stands up and raises his pint. "Not going to lie, we were worried about you during the hike, Jacob. But you made it!"

My face is burning.

Jack continues, "Bro, we all agree, you're one of the big dawgs. We're honored to officially induct you as the newest member of 5:30 Nation! To Silverstein! Cheers!" I smile bashfully and pinch myself under the table to make sure this isn't a dream.

Everyone raises their mugs. "To Silverstein!"

People stop eating, and it feels like the entire pub is staring at me. The place is packed, filled with about a hundred tired, windburned, and weary hikers.

I wave my hand at Jack, modestly deflecting the attention away. All I can muster is, "Oh, it was nothing." A voice in my head says, *Dude, could you possibly give a lamer response?*

Vance, sitting to my left, pats me on the back. I've worked so hard to fit in with the group and be one of the dudes, and now that they're honoring me into their fraternity, the attention is more than anticipated. I can't handle it. I just want to be alone. I want to crawl under the table to hide my embarrassment. Instead, I grab Sean's menu and bury my head in the entrée list.

I'm relieved when our server—a blonde surfer dude who's a long way from the ocean—sidles up. "What can I get you to drink?"

My reflex is to always tell servers I don't drink. The waitstaff walks away pissed, knowing their tip's cut in half. But when I see the faces of 5:30 Nation eagerly awaiting my beverage order, I give in to the non-verbal peer pressure. *When in Rome!* "I'll have what he ordered," I say, pointing to Barlow.

"Good choice, Silverstein!" Barlow shouts from down the table.

"And give me the Lone Pine Burger!"

"That's what I'm having too!" Barlow exclaims.

"We're twinning!" I say, and immediately kick myself for such a juvenile response.

Before I can hide my face back in the menu (even though I already ordered), I hear laughter across the table, and Teddy says, "Classic! My daughters are always twinning. Love that!"

I put the menu down. I really *am* ingrained in 5:30 Nation! I grab a handful of nachos and crispy fried brussels sprouts and dump them on my plate. I lean back in my chair and appreciate how kind the whole group has been to me. I finally feel like I belong!

I tune out the conversations around me and go deep into my head to mediate the voices having a field day.

My inner child is bursting with pride. *We're finally being recognized, but we don't deserve it!*

My rational side scolds him: *Don't ruin our moment. Just soak it in. We do deserve this. Remember in middle school when you wondered if anyone would notice if we vanished and never came home from school? Those distant memories were thoughts of a kid who never felt heard. You're being heard now.*

The inner child won't give up so easily. *Come on, those images still resurface!* The inner child is right. Morbid thoughts still creep into my rational mind on the drive home from the office. If I never made it home for dinner, would I be missed? Would the endless conversations about the day's dramas continue if I wasn't present to hear them? Would the family just move on without me?

Rational me looks up and sees the animated, smiling faces sitting around him at the table. He knows the inner child is trying to play tricks on him. The truth—there in front of us all along—was the unequivocal answer to that universal question: *Of course I would be missed.*

It's time for my inner child to grow up. Newfound confidence compels me to speak.

I spontaneously stand up at the head of the table and raise my beer mug. "Fellas, I've felt like an outsider my entire life.

I've never been the cool jock, the talented musician, or the good-looking theater kid. I've always been the geek—the awkward, shy, and studious one who worked hard for good grades."

The whole pub is staring at me again, but this time I don't care. It's my time to be heard. "What I'm trying to say is that you've welcomed me to 5:30 Nation with open arms and, more importantly, without judgment. It may not be a big deal to you all, but including this dorky dude from Connecticut as one of your own on your mountain odyssey, has been one of the best experiences in my life. It's been an honor and a privilege to hike with you to the summit of Mt. Whitney and back." I stick out my stein and raise it high above my head. "To 5:30 Nation." I bring the beer to my mouth, and the froth of Lone Pine Lager feels cold against my dry lips. It's the best tasting beer I've ever had!

Our table returns my toast, "To 5:30 Nation!"

The whole pub erupts in cheers and echoes back, "To 5:30 Nation!"

Chapter 19 – No (Middle-Aged) Man's Land

Back at my hotel, I'm lying in bed wearing shorts and a T-shirt but, despite my light apparel, I'm sweating profusely. My whole body is shaking. The Advil I just took has not kicked in yet.

I text Barlow. (My cell phone's finally working again.) *I feel like I'm dying. I don't know what's wrong with me.*

He texts me back: *be over in a sec.*

It takes all I have to lift myself out of bed and let Barlow into my room.

My old friend never minces words: "Dude, you look like shit."

"I *feel* like shit," I groan, wiping the sweat off my forehead and crawling back into bed. "I make it up and down Whitney unscathed only to croak in the hotel room! Oh, the irony!"

Barlow ignores my melodrama, puts down his Diet Mountain Dew, and brings me a bottle of water from my minifridge. "Keep hydrating. You probably sweated more than you ever have in your life. And you didn't drink enough water at dinner."

His soda makes a lightbulb go off. "Hey," I say as Barlow pulls out the chair next to the desk and sits down, "I never drink caffeine, and I had *two* energy drinks on the mountain." I try to keep my teeth from chattering. "Maybe I'm coming down from a caffeine and adrenaline high."

"Are you for real? *No* caffeine? You're, like, from another planet! But what does that have to do with the price of tea in China?" Barlow stares at me compassionately. "You're probably just coming down from a binger. You had three beers tonight—I bet you're not used to being drunk!"

"I feel horrible. Make it stop!" I whine.

"You've just got to ride it out. Like that time I detoxed after snorting coke in Vegas at Jack's bachelor party."

"*Cocaine?*" I ask incredulously, like a kid finding out about his father's affair.

"Don't be such a straight lace, Silverstein. I mean, who hasn't done drugs?"

"Well, me, for one," I whisper, like someone will hear me and I'll be kicked out of 5:30 Nation.

"Of course you haven't, but that's a discussion for another day. Let me get you some cold towels for your forehead. You're drenched in sweat."

Channeling his inner nurse, Barlow goes to the bathroom and comes back with a damp washcloth. He wraps it up like a bandana and gently places it on my forehead. He's a good friend, and I love him like a brother.

I thank him, and maybe it's because I feel weak and uninhibited after our seventeen-hour hike (or perhaps I just want to distract myself from the chills) that I ask, "Is it ridiculous that a middle-aged man would want to fit in and ascend Whitney with you guys? To challenge myself and do something I've never done before? To be one of the cool kids for once?"

Barlow looks at me with empathy in his eyes. "No. I don't think it's ridiculous at all. We should never stop giving ourselves a license to dream."

"Really?"

"Yeah. Age is just a construct. Never feel constrained by how old you are. You should never stop challenging yourself. Why does there have to be such a stigma about middle age?"

"What do you mean?"

"It's funny you mentioned this because I've been thinking about aging lately." Barlow rests his elbows on the armchair and presses his fingertips together.

The Advil is finally kicking in. I'm feeling better, and I want to hear more about Barlow's philosophy. "Go on."

"There's a gap in society for middle-aged guys like us. We've passed all the memorable milestones in our lives, like college, finding a career, getting married and having kids. Other than family milestones, it's like we're on autopilot—breakfast, work, dinner, and sleep. Rinse and repeat. The only thing we've got left is retirement. Kind of depressing, if you think about it."

I shake my head at Barlow and respond, "That's pretty cynical. There's still so much for us to experience with our families."

Barlow takes a swig of his Diet Dew. "If what I'm saying isn't true, then why are you here on this trip with us?"

"I already told you why."

"C'mon, if you were fulfilled and content, you wouldn't be here."

Touché. Barlow got me. "That's a good point. I did need this trip."

"You know I'm a big pop-culture guy, and what I'm saying is totally reflected in our culture. Think about it, even Hollywood couldn't care less about us!"

"Explain."

"You've got your coming-of-age flicks like *The Breakfast Club*, and your rom-coms with hot twenty-somethings, and then it's straight to *Driving Miss Daisy*. There's no market for middle-aged guys like us."

"Unless you're a *40-Year-Old Virgin*."

Barlow laughs. "We're in no-man's land," he declares.

I nod, impressed with Barlow's well thought out thesis. "I get what you're saying. There's a void in pop-culture for average dudes our age."

Barlow stretches his arms out and yawns.

"Am I boring you?" I ask.

"No. The hike and the beers are catching up with me. I'm beat." Barlow looks at his watch. I take another sip of water to fill the silence.

My good buddy slowly lifts himself off the chair. "It was such an awesome time. I'm really glad you came." I'm too tired to get up and give him a hug, but Barlow reaches out his hand, and I grasp it. "Love you, bro," he says with sincerity.

"Love you too, Barlow." I swallow hard, the words we've just said to each other solidifying our evening bromance.

Barlow starts to close the door and then peeks his head back in, "Silverstein, I saw you reinvent yourself today, and it was awesome! Never stop growing!"

The red LED lights on the digital clock read 11:11 p.m. I am left to ponder Barlow's parting words about how a coming-of-*middle-age* genre isn't a thing. My trek with 5:30 Nation shows it *can* be a thing when you get out there and experience what life has to offer. You don't have to be a movie star or write a bestseller to have something important to say!

Chapter 20 – HunBun's Home

I pull into the garage and breathe a sigh of relief. Home at last! I'm more than exhausted. The flight back to Connecticut and the lack of sleep on the plane have caught up with me. I can barely keep my eyes open as I dream of crawling into bed next to Leah.

I press the button to close the garage door and step into my house. It's 1:35 a.m. A wave of warmth washes over me. There's nothing better than the comfort of home. I whisper to myself, "It's so good to be back!" I tiptoe into the mudroom so I don't wake anyone at this ungodly hour. Leah hates a mess, so as quietly as I can, I bring my backpack and luggage upstairs to the laundry room. I'll unload and wash my clothes tomorrow.

I walk into the kitchen, and the silence is deafening. I start to regret choosing an evening flight, because my late arrival at home means there is no Leah to greet me with a big kiss and no children jumping into my arms. (My wife is a stickler for bedtime.)

I traverse the stairs slowly, wishing there was a celebration for me like the New York Yankees going through the Canyon of Heroes after a World Series win. I stop in front of the girls' room. Although Leah and I made a pact that we would never disturb the girls while they're sleeping, I can't resist peeking my head into their room. When Rina was having a tough time going to bed, Autumn agreed to move out of her own room to become her big sister's roommate. They are sound asleep, so I walk in, and when I see my vulnerable, adorable girls snuggling together in bed (they're often bedmates too!), I feel happy, content, and whole. I hover over their bed, holding my breath so I don't wake them. I lean over and lay a soft kiss on each of their cheeks. Although I'm not a religious man, I find it comforting to say a silent prayer in my head. *Thank you, God, for bestowing these girls in my life. Bless them.* I figure it can't hurt, just in case anyone out there is listening. I'm so looking forward to seeing their big, beautiful eyes tomorrow morning and giving them gigantic bear hugs! I almost can't contain my jubilation.

I enter my bedroom and decide I'll brush my teeth in the morning, so I walk to the side of my bed and strip to my boxers. Despite it being so quiet you could have heard a pin drop, Leah wakes up as I pull the covers back so I can slide in next to her.

"Welcome home, HunBuns," she whispers.

I lean over and give her a gentle kiss on the cheek not buried in her pillow.

"How was it?"

I can't possibly sum up my life-reaffirming journey in one sentence, so I table the discussion. "I'll tell you all about it tomorrow when you're awake. But it was incredible! It's great to be home! I love you."

She leans over and kisses me on the lips. "I'm glad you made it back safely. Can't wait to hear about it. Love you too."

I wrap the sheets over my head and breathe in the fresh scent of fabric softener. It smells like home. Before I close my eyes, I realize I'd better pee before I hit the hay.

I walk into the bathroom and turn on the lights so I don't miss the bowl. (Leah hates it when I splatter pee all over the place, which will certainly lead to an unpleasant morning). After I empty my bladder, I fill my glass with water, take a sip, and that's when I see the homemade sign on the mirror behind my sink:

Welcome Home Daddy! We Missed You!!
Love, Mommy, Rina, and Autumn

The sign instantly puts everything in perspective. I drop to my knees and start crying like a lost kid who finally finds their mom after getting lost in the department store.

Despite Mark's lament about loving the peace and quiet of being at home alone, seeing Leah, the girls, and their sign has cleared my mind and filled me with joy. I went out west to prove I could climb Mt. Whitney and be *one of the guys,* but I didn't realize being away would awaken the family man in me. I'm *now* with the people I cherish most in the world; they accept me for who I am, and this is where I have the deepest love, affection, and comfort. It was fun to be an honorary 5:30 Nation bro, but my real tribe is my family, right here in Matingly, Connecticut.

They say, "Home is where the heart is," and it must be true, because this home that Leah and I have built together is where my heart has always been.

Acknowledgements

I would like to thank those who have been instrumental in helping me make *Conquering Whitney: A Mountain of Misadventure* a reality. Much gratitude to DJ Schuette for his patience, guidance, and commitment throughout this writing journey. Ali Boa, who's editing, energy, and enthusiasm for this project came when it was needed the most. Romuald Dzemo at The Book Commentary brought his special skillset to enhance the book, and Daniela Kinsbourne's artistic vision made the cover come to life. Shira Langberg deserves recognition for creating the mountain image at the start of each chapter.

Thank you to Julie Sarkissian and the Westport Writer's Workshop for providing me with the spark to start writing again! I am very fortunate to have this first-class organization nearby to offer encouragement and mentorship during my writing process.

Every engine needs fuel to keep going, and I'm grateful for everyone who kept fueling me with encouragement to tell this story: Sandra Bendfeldt, Debbie Frishman, Jaclyn Gilbert, Josh Hyman, John Schod, Rahul Shah, Craig Sherter, and Todd Walkow.

Most importantly, a special shout-out goes to my wife, Rachel, for being the best partner in life you could ask for, and to my three daughters who are my beacon of light when times get dark. I don't always get to say this out loud, but I appreciate my parents, Phyllis and David Langberg, and my sister, Rebecca Weinstein, for always supporting me during my journey.